VAMPIRES DON'T BABYSIT

VAMPIRE MYTHICALS BOOK 1

CANDICE GILMER

FLIRTATION PUBLISHING
WICHITA, KS

VAMPIRES DON'T BABYSIT
COPYRIGHT © 2019 BY CANDICE GILMER
COVER BY FLIRTATION DESIGNS
ISBN: 9781091251694

FIRST PUBLICATION: 2019

10 9 8 7 6 5 4 3 2 1

SURVIVING SHOULD HAVE BEEN ENOUGH

IT WASN'T

Jake Reynolds and his fellow vampires survived the slaughter of their master, Melios, at the hands of the Immortal Knights Templar.

Call it luck. Call it fate. Call it whatever the hell you want.

Jake just knows that he should have been dead—another pile of sooty ash on the ground. Now he must find his place in the mythical world—vampires aren't the only ones out there.

Even his doctor is a super-hot werewolf. He's not entirely sure he should find her sexy, but he does. And he wants to see if wolves and vamps are compatible.

In all the ways.

But the world's a chaotic mess, and he's been tasked to help fix it. Penance for previous crimes. They do what they're told, and go where they have to, learning to live without being monsters among men. And kick-ass, occasionally, in the name of Jackstone Foundation.

But when The Kid—Melios's pet—needs help, Jake will not leave her out in the cold. She fed him too many times on the sly to leave her hanging now.

Mythicals are coming for her. And it's up to Jake to keep her safe.

But what can one lone vampire do against an army and an ancient bloodline?

PROLOGUE

There is a moment in every man's life, where he must evaluate his choices. Determine if he's really made the right ones. Put his faith in the right place.

Former Sergeant First Class Jake Reynolds fucked up.

Seriously fucked up.

Because, nope, he didn't put his faith in the right place.

He realized this as pain shot through him from someone attempting to hit him with a sword.

He jerked and jumped out of the way, the wound aching.

Then, like a physical slap upside the head, Reynolds felt an explosive release of pressure in his mind. Or in his heart maybe? Maybe some of both? His humanity sort of started to seep through his body as if it were gas or liquid being poured into his soul.

Then the pain hit. This was a new kind of pain.

Not the pain of battle, but something else.

He shook his head, trying to get rid of it, but it only amplified. Where was he? What was going on?

Confused.

What, where?

He was in battle.

Fighting for his master…

A vampire.

What. The. Hell.

He hesitated. Thoughts ran rampant, like a seeing his life pass before his eyes.

But it wasn't his life. It was his new life. New death. Bridge to immortality—that's what Melios had called it. A bridge to a never-ending existence, where not only would he never die, but he'd be the top of the food chain.

He'd be a monster among men.

A king.

It had seemed right at the time.

Looking back, it was obvious Jake Reynolds had really, really, really fucked up.

Something hit him. He winced. He swung back to block it. Was he armed? Did he have any kind of weapon?

A curved blade he used to block his attacker.

He glanced around the room.

A moment's clarity.

Sort of.

Immortal Knights Templar slaughtered vampires around him without hesitation. People who had been his companions. Friends—almost—were disappearing in bursts of smoke and ash, right before his eyes.

The pain swelled in his head.

His gaze darted to his team. They all had been soldiers in their lives before this one, and they all winced, almost simultaneously.

Then they all paused.

Looked to him.

As a soldier does, when unsure of what to do, they look to a commanding officer.

Reynolds had only one recourse.

"Surrender," he said, dropping to the ground, hands out. "We surrender." He dropped his blade and fell to knees.

His head thundered in pain, like the worst migraine in the world, and he wobbled as he went down.

The Templar swinging the broadsword at him paused and redirected the heavy metal weapon, and the blade came down within inches of his face.

"How interesting," he said, a bit of a British accent to him. "How very interesting."

TWO WEEKS LATER

The klaxons went off, alerting the Immortal Knights Templar of an incoming attack.

Sir Richard de Lyons charged for the front door. Security protocols instigated, and everyone at the compound began executing their tasks. Every Templar Knight knew their place. Every staff member. All knew what to do in an attack, and where to go.

It was part of the drills.

Or perhaps, after seven hundred years, they all just knew.

Tonight, though was not a drill.

Richard reached the front door, met by Sir Adrian de Pairaud. Richard hit the perimeter lights. He handed the broadsword sitting by the entrance to Adrian and put his hand on his own samurai sword.

"What is it?" Adrian asked.

"Vampires," Richard replied. He didn't have to look. He knew.

They came.

The vision he'd had only a few weeks ago was coming to pass.

In exacting detail.

Vampires were descending on the Templar compound in ferocious numbers. He counted at least a dozen he could see.

Which meant there were a lot more he couldn't see.

"How close do we let them get," Adrian asked.

Richard flipped on the ultraviolet lights on the compound's exteriors. A couple of vampires who'd been moving in got hit with the light.

It burned them just enough that they backed off. Not enough to kill the vampires, but enough to keep them from moving in faster than the Templars wanted.

"Porch. We'll have the high ground."

Adrian smirked.

"What?" Richard asked.

"Nothing. Pop culture reference," Adrian replied. "Though it could very much apply."

Richard raised his eyebrow. "Not the time."

"Right." Adrian nodded. "You take the right, I'll go left, and we'll slow them down."

"The rearguard in place?"

"They're getting there," he said.

Richard nodded. The two of them could slow the influx down, prevent them from getting inside. And then—

"Richard?" came the kid's voice.

Richard glanced over his shoulder at the stairs.

The speaker really wasn't a kid anymore. At least, she didn't look it. She'd probably always be tiny—a life of never getting enough to eat would do that to a growing kid. But she was starting to fill out, to look more like her actual age. Older than he'd thought originally when he'd found her.

But she still had those eyes.

Eyes that belonged to someone else.

Making this tween a conundrum that no one saw coming.

She had clapped her hands over her ears, fear in her violet eyes. "Richard? What is happening?"

"I'm here," Richard said, heading to the stairs where she looked for him. "It's okay. I'm here."

Adrian locked in braces on the windows to prevent any of the vampires from coming in and getting around Richard and Adrian's frontal defense. Staff ran back and forth, preparing for the invasion about to happen.

"Richard!" she cried out when she saw him. The girl got closer. "What's going on, I thought I'd be safe." The fear shifted to anger. "You said I'd be safe! You're a liar!"

"You will be," Richard replied, crossing to her.

"No!" Anger swirled with the fear, and she looked ready to fight.

Richard gritted his teeth. "No. Stop! Now is not the time! You need to get to the safe room."

"No!"

Adrian jarred his attention. "Look at the size of that guy."

Richard glanced out the nearest window. "They're hitting us hard."

Adrian grimaced as an unusually large vampire landed in their front lawn. "What do they want? We took out the nest. There aren't any of those vampires left, are there?"

Richard started walking the girl back toward the safe rooms, and she kept protesting, her voice noise against the attacking background of the vampires slamming into parts of the house.

"There were a few left behind. They're in Jackstone," Richard said, directed toward Adrian.

But the girl stopped and spun to face Richard. "Some of Melios's men are in Jackstone?" the girl asked, her eyes wide. "I wanna see them! I want to know who it is."

"Later," Richard replied.

And he thought about it. The girl had lived in Melios's

nest for years—a pet of the mad vampire's of a sort. She knew many of the vampires. At least, who played for what teams.

He took her hand. "Come here."

She nodded and followed him to the window nearest the door.

"Do you know them?" He asked, gesturing out at the horde of vampires building up outside. They were gathering their numbers just at the ring of light beyond the porch. The ultraviolet lights would keep them off the porch until they were ready for them.

She pushed the thin curtain back just enough to peer through. And she shook her head. "They're not Melios's vampires. They look mean."

"If they're not from Melios, then who?" Adrian asked.

One got so close as to get to the foot of the stairs, wincing against the light.

Richard saw an emblem on the shirt the vampire wore. He knew that symbol. And it wasn't a good sign.

The girl inhaled a breath. "They're old. Like way older than most of Melios's nest. I recognize the crest, but I can't think of where."

Richard pushed her away from the window. "Kid, back up."

She took a few steps back. "What do they want?"

Richard glanced at her. "Probably you. Go, kid."

Her eyes got wide, and she nodded.

Gunshots echoed outside.

The black lights were destroyed.

Like a freight train blast, outside the porch thundered with dozens of vampires storming the compound.

The door flew open.

"Go now!" Richard stabbed his sword through the first

vampire through the door. Ash went everywhere. And three more were behind him, pushing through.

He and Adrian attempted to keep them bottle-necked here. From the left, some glass broke. There went any strategy.

Unfortunately, Richard knew it wasn't the best-laid plan. And it was only going to get worse.

"Richard! Come with me!" she cried.

"No, kid. Go."

She ran away, and he heard a door shut in the distance.

He hoped it was her getting secured in the safe room.

Vampires were practically falling from the sky and coming in from everywhere. Angry, pissed off, old vampires.

Yeah. This was going to take a while.

1

SIX WEEKS LATER

"*And* how are the baby vampires today?" James Henrick, the owner of this facility, asked as he walked toward the bay of hospital beds in the basement of Jackstone Foundation.

His pale skin looked unusually warm, and his light eyes sparkled.

Vampires tended to glow right after they fed, or so Doctor Megan Criger had always noticed. She shifted from foot to foot, waiting for James to reach her. She glanced at the room of vampires she'd just been checking on.

Though she didn't have anything spectacular to report.

She had been about to return to her rounds upstairs when she heard footsteps.

One whiff of the air and she'd known who was approaching.

Vampires had a distinct odor, and James Henrick was no exception, though he tried to hide it with cologne.

Yeah, the co-owner of Jackstone Foundation, one of the largest charity organizations in the world, was a bloodsucker.

It should be kinda funny.

If one didn't know exactly what James Henrick and his partner, Joseph Oliver, did for the mythical community, as well as the human one.

Megan did, though.

She'd been with the company for a few years now. So, she could say, with a decent amount of certainty, that yes, she knew what Jackstone Foundation was really up to.

Most of the time, she approved.

Today, however, she walked the line between approval and disgust.

She brushed her bangs over. Her widow's peak—the sign of being a werewolf—probably appeared for a moment but then disappeared behind her hair. That's why she kept the bangs. Prevented the humans from commenting on the perfect point on her brow, and it kept the mythicals from recognizing her as one of their own.

She looked back through the window to the large hospital room, where six vampires laid in shiny white beds. The only color in the room was the banks of monitors behind each bed that displayed each patient's current physical and mental activity.

Though there wasn't much going on there.

She had the results displayed on her tablet as well, so she didn't have to actually go in there with them to check their readings.

Thank the stars.

She was not a fan of bloodsuckers. In fact, she really didn't know why they were still alive at all. The Immortal Templar Knights, who policed mythical activities all over the world, were not known to take prisoners. Dozens were killed that night.

So why these six were saved, she had no idea.

Yet here they were, mostly alive.

For now, anyway.

She glanced at her readings, but really, they hadn't changed.

She wasn't sure if they ever would.

"Their wounds were bad, but the real damage was in their minds." She shifted from one foot to the other. "I don't know what that old vampire did to them, I've never seen anything quite like it. The coma they're all in," she said as she shook her head. "I've done all I can for them. I've seen the psychic suggestion some vampires can do, but this is something else. We won't know if the control is permanent until they wake. If they wake."

And that was the gist of it—would they wake at all? Were they wasting their time and resources trying to take care of them? Because the chance of them actually waking up, well, it was getting slimmer by the day.

The Jackstone CEO nodded. "Melios was very talented with mind manipulation. I wouldn't be surprised if he learned a few new tricks over the centuries."

Megan—in her head, anyway—smirked. "Evidence suggests he had learned more than just a few new tricks." She glanced at her vampire boss. The man's face was stern, his dark hair neat and tidy.

He looked every bit the professional. As long as one didn't notice how light his eyes were. It was the tell-tale sign of his true vampire nature.

While not a huge fan of vampires, Megan was able to work for this one, probably because he never really bothered her. She was very rarely questioned about anything she did in the medical wing and was paid generously for her expertise in mythical medicine.

Not every doctor who specialized in mythical medicine got to study on the island of Avalon. The magically-enchanted island was home to all types of mythical creatures.

Megan worked her ass off to get her scholarships there. Now, almost a decade later, she was one of the best doctors in the world. But like all mythicals, humans might know *who* she was, but not what she was. Not really, anyway.

So, she patched up mythicals who were brought in for treatment and ran the medical wing as she saw fit.

This group of vampires, though, brought James down to the unit more often than usual.

And he asked more questions than he ever had before.

He took a step closer to the glass, his gaze moving from one bed to the other. "Will it be lasting damage to their minds?"

"We won't know until they wake. Typically though, when the master dies, any mind control ceases. This is different, though. Even the brainwaves are different." She didn't know how else to explain it.

The way the brains were firing in there—and they were firing, no mistaking that—it wasn't typical for vampires.

She wasn't sure what they were going to get when they woke.

"Do you think they'll still be loyal to Melios after they wake?"

The fine hairs on her arms twitched like they wanted to shift and grow and turn into a wolf. Right here, right now.

She sighed.

Because she was almost sure she knew what he wanted with them.

While her boss and his partner, Joseph Oliver, and now their trinity mate, Nicole Bernard owned Jackstone Foundation—the most powerful mythical charity in the world—they were not friends of many vampires.

Megan had no idea why they created Jackstone Foundation, but the company helped those in need, whether they were human or mythical. Humans, who'd been hurt because of mythicals, and mythicals who needed to relocate, or medical assistance.

There were a lot of mythicals didn't approve of the foundation's activities.

"No idea," she finally said. It was an accurate enough answer to the question. "Their brains are fighting with themselves. Mental manipulation is more than just hypnotizing someone. It's also giving the target exactly what they've always wanted. Or showing them what they already believe is true, because someone else believes it too."

James nodded. "Melios was a powerful vampire—one of the oldest still in existence. His bloodline went back to some of the first vampire families. He'd held, well, many vampires under his spell for years, convinced of their superiority in the world. To think he could do this to a group of soldiers is not unreasonable."

"What do you mean, soldiers?"

"They all had military backgrounds. Melios called him his animals. His Seals."

"Were they Navy Seals, then?"

He shook his head. "I think some were, but these six, I don't know. Melios just clumped them all together."

"How do you know that?" she asked.

"I was there." James put his hand on the glass that allowed him and Dr. Criger to see the vampires in the room.

Whoa, he'd been there?

Megan had heard about the big battle almost two months ago, between vampires, werewolves, and the Immortal Knights Templar. But she didn't know the CEO was part of the melee.

Must have been a hell of a fight.

"This seems extreme, though, even for Melios. No one would have anticipated he would have such a blatant mind-control-manipulation over so many young vampires at one time."

Megan watched him. "He was up to something. And I have to wonder if you are as well."

James glanced at her. "Why?"

"Why are they alive? You and I both know Immortal Templars are merciless. They rarely dig deeper; they just kill the offender at the moment."

He nodded.

"So, what are you doing with these vampires, Mister Henrick?"

"Nothing at the moment, they're all in comas." He smiled as though he was trying to sell her something.

It only made her hackles stand up even more.

A nurse came down the hall, one Megan had been working with for a while now, and on her more interesting cases, she always had Amy as part of the team. With almost as much mythical knowledge as Megan had, Amy had proven her value around mythical patients. As she approached the room, she nodded to Megan and smiled at James, before heading inside.

James nodded back to her, a friendly smile on his face.

"Who is that?" James asked. "I don't recognize her."

Megan opened her mouth. "Amy. Moved here from Avalon."

"Avalon? Did you know her?" James raised his eyebrow. They both watched as the nurse approached the first bed, checking the vitals, adjusting bedding, and generally caring for the nearest vampire.

"No," Megan replied. "I may have gone to school there, but that didn't mean I knew everyone on the island." Everyone outside of Avalon seemed to think the place was a little bitty town where everyone knew everyone, and they all had Sunday dinner together every week.

As if.

"Fair enough," he replied. "Is she magical?"

Megan shook her head. "Retired Fairy."

He smiled. "Fascinating. I've always wanted to get to know a fairy. They say they have a scent to them that is magnetic for corporeal mythicals."

"That's just in the movies." Megan rolled her eyes. "Was there more, sir?"

His gaze remained on the vampires, attention away from the nurse, and his expression softened. "I want to help them exist in the real world." There was something in his expression, genuine sorrow for the vampires. "Do things to better the world, not hurt it."

She nodded because she understood what James was up to. "I hope we can save them."

Each vampire's chest rose and fell. The monitors were typical, nothing out of the ordinary. Blood was fed to them intravenously. Their coloring looked better than it had a few weeks before, but they remained unconscious.

"If we cannot, then..." his words trailed off, and he glanced at her.

"I will not kill them," she blurted out. She'd spent her adult life learning how to be a doctor for mythicals and humans. She'd taken an oath, just like any human doctor would take—to do no harm.

And in her case, as a doctor of mythicals—her oath was to not kill, or she would be subject to the same fate. It was one of the biggest inconsistencies of mythical law versus human. Humans prosecuted others for killing, jailed them, and basically kept them around for years.

In the mythical world, if a mythical vanished, he was likely dead. If the killer was caught, the killer would wind up a pile of ashy soot somewhere, blowing in the wind. Some thought the fact that all mythicals disappeared into ash was a safeguard to keep humans from detecting their existence and finding remains.

Others believed it was a divine joke, showing how much the mythicals didn't matter in the world.

Some mythicals still honored their dead. Just like humans did. Many, however, did not. Megan was one who did not. While she would spend her days saving a mythical's life, if his death is upon him, then there is nothing to be done. No resuscitation. No coming back.

Death is forever.

James raised his eyebrow. "I didn't ask you to."

She fiddled with the tablet in her arms. "You were going to."

He shook his head. "If it comes to that, I have a plan."

"Which is?"

"I have a sheldevak."

The doctor inhaled a breath. Lovely, because that's the last being she wanted to deal with. "I see." She glanced at her tablet and back at the room.

Amy was moving from bed to bed, nothing looked any different.

Yet all of a sudden, readings started flashing.

What in the world?

She tapped the tablet, harder than necessary, thinking it might actually be able to change the readings she was getting. Her gaze darted from the tablet to the room.

Amy.

No one had moved.

Nothing.

"What do you see?"

"Increased brain function."

"Which one?"

She glanced at him. "All of them." She moved toward the door to check them out.

"Amy," she said as she moved.

The nurse seemed to realize that something was going on. She'd made it to the far side and was standing near the bed of the largest vampire.

Oh no...

Surely not all of them were waking now, at the same time.

One step.

Two steps.

And the room, which had been nothing but sleeping vampires exploded in movement and yells and screams.

The largest one had Amy in a vice grip.

"Seal that door," James said. "Don't let them escape!"

"Amy!"

The nurse punched and kicked at the vampire that now had her by the throat.

Megan reached for the door's panel to seal it. They had to contain them before—

But it was too late.

The door burst open, the metal flying off the tracks, and she ducked out of the way, barely missing the flying panel.

Two of the vampires erupted from the room.

Flew.

Or just leaped in that very powerful way that vampires did.

"Shit," James muttered. He hit his watch, calling for security. "I need a Cold Team downstairs immediately. Seal off the basement. Now."

2

*C*haos exploded around Jake Reynolds.

Lights flashed, painfully bright, shining through his closed eyelids.

Yelling.

Screams.

War...

He snapped his eyes open.

White.

White everywhere.

He bolted up. Movement all around him.

Someone leaped and knocked over metal. Clattering and clanking. Cursing.

Voices. Voices he recognized.

He blinked a few times, trying to focus in the blinding white. Everything was so bright and overwhelming. What in the world was all of this?

No, this wasn't the afterlife. This was still life. Existence.

Whatever you wanted to call it now. Not the human version, but life, anyway.

His head still hurt, but he forced himself up.

Just in time to see two blurs take off down the hall, moving faster than should have been possible. But he saw them.

A man and a woman. Shapes that even in his not-quite-focused state, he recognized.

He sighed.

Of course, Travis and Joanie ran off. They were always together.

Pieces in his mind started to fall back together.

The fight at Melios's building, the one with the Immortal Knights Templar and the werewolves.

What had happened again? Why were they there?

A woman.

Melios had kidnapped some woman, who was mated to someone, who knew where someone else was...

Bullshit, overall. And a stupid-assed plan that was based on lust and greed. He'd wanted to tell Melios that when they'd been waiting for the attack to come. But Melios was not known for listening very well.

Especially not to him. Jake was just one of Melios's good little troopers. A soldier who became a vampire.

One of the old vampire's pets.

He gritted his teeth. Not the first time Jake Reynolds regretted his choices the last decade or so.

He'd survived somehow. Why he wasn't a pile of ash on the ground, he didn't know.

Who else had made it? Did anyone else escape the battle?

Besides Travis and Joanie? In the nest, he'd brought together a handful of other newly turned vampires into his own little team, creating a special forces group for the vampire king. If that's what he was.

That's sure how Melios acted.

They'd become a family that could all bond over their

shared human experiences. And find a life in the eternal night of vampirism. Or some such bullshit.

Something crashed. What now?

He took a quick inventory in the room. Five beds. Two of which still had people in them. Isaac Malcomb was next to him, and past that, was Edward Thompson. On the far end, would have been Deke Smith.

Were the colossal vampire not on his feet, growling.

Fuck.

The biggest of all of them, Smith, held a woman against him in one hand and was hurling medical equipment with the other.

Fluid sprayed everywhere from IV's being ripped out. Broken glass and mechanical stuff, and a haze of burning-computer-flared fire.

In the middle, a monster on the rampage.

"Let go of me," the woman in nursing scrubs cried. "Stop it right now!"

Deke growled. "You cannot stop me! I can do anything!" He bellowed.

"Will you knock it off," snarled Isaac Malcomb said, rubbing his eyes as he sat up. "Can I not wake up for five minutes in quiet? Do you have to—" Malcomb turned to look at Smith. "What the fuck Deke?"

Jake climbed off the bed, his energy pumping, adrenalin beginning to flow.

Handle this situation.

"Let her go, Deke."

"Fuck all you." Deke leaned in. "I am powerful!" He pulled the woman into him. And the bastard bared his fangs. "Feel the energy! The power!"

Leaned down.

Lust and power in his eyes.

"Oh, hell no," Jake said, taking a couple of steps. "At ease, soldier!"

"Fuck you, Reynolds. You're not the boss of me. Not anymore." He clamped down.

The woman screamed.

"You will follow orders, Soldier!" Jake bellowed back, closing in on Deke.

"Fuck. You." Deke spat, blood on his face, puncture marks on the woman's neck seeping blood.

Malcomb came up behind him, monitor in his hands and slammed Deke upside the head.

He growled.

Spun.

Attacked Malcomb.

The woman fell to the floor. Jake plowed through the chaos, heading toward the nurse, but stopped, hung up by IVs in his arms.

"Damn," he muttered and jerked the lines out. More fluid sprayed everywhere.

She flailed around like she was hunting for something in the drawers nearby.

He ran to the woman's side and pulled her away from Malcomb and Smith.

"Soldiers! Attention!" he tried again.

Malcomb paused.

Smith didn't.

He landed a hard punch in Malcomb's face.

"Fuck!" Malcomb cried out. "Smith you're a goddamn idiot!"

"Power! Feel the power!" He growled again. Like he was a goddamn monster. Though really, Deke kinda was, compared to the others.

Jake turned to assess the woman's condition. "Ma'am." Blood dripped down her neck where Deke had bitten her.

He stared at it for a moment.

Then grabbed a cloth from a drawer. "Here," he said, pressing it to the nurse.

A drop got on his hand.

Usually, the scent made him ravenous. Desperate.

Seeing it? Ten times worse.

Touching it like that? He was done for.

The blood smelled as divine, and his usual, knee-jerk reaction was to leap for it. To eat when it was available because he didn't know when he'd get to eat again.

It was the same for all of them. They were always ready to ravage whatever blood was available. That is when they weren't under orders to stand there and watch others eat.

One of Melios's little mind games. He loved testing their discipline.

Yet today, even seeing the woman's blood, he didn't attack her. It was on his hand, and he didn't want to taste it.

He wasn't hungry.

He wasn't hungry.

He couldn't remember the last time he didn't feel hungry. Even at war, he always found something to eat. And he actually felt, well, kind of good. He didn't feel ravenously starving and ready to blow up the world.

"What the hell is wrong with you two," Edward Thompson snarled and leaped into the fray between Smith and Malcomb. As tall as Smith, but not quite as thick, Thompson would kick about anyone's ass if needed. But no one was as large as Smith.

"He's trying to eat a nurse," Reynolds snapped as he helped the nurse adjust the bandages on her throat.

"I am fine, thank you," she said, her voice laced with a soft British accent.

Smith punched at Malcomb and Thompson. "Did you

smell her?" Each of his punches made connections, making Malcomb and Thompson stumble.

"She smelled divine."

"Doesn't mean you can just take a bite of her," Reynolds clapped back.

"Like hell," Smith said, charging toward Reynolds and the down nurse.

Malcomb glanced at Thompson.

The two got a hold of Smith, one on either side. "Calm down," Malcomb yelled.

Smith took a breath, almost dragging the two of them with him for a second. And yelled. "No!"

The sound, a mini shockwave that blasted so much force and energy, more equipment fell over.

Good god! Since when could vampires do that? And why the fuck was Smith able to do it all?

"Smith, stand down," Reynolds yelled, getting in front of Smith. His voice was not nearly so powerful.

He paused for a second and waited.

Smith jerked away from Thompson and Malcomb.

"No." Smith puffed his chest out and slammed into Reynolds.

Reynolds met the larger man, toe for toe, and didn't move. "I am your commanding officer." Of course, he was about six inches shorter, but he wasn't intimidated by Deke Smith.

A bully, if Reynolds ever met one.

"Not anymore," Smith curled back. His gaze flickered to the side. Jake immediately knew he'd glanced at the nurse.

"No, you will not."

"You gonna stop me?" Smith glanced around at everyone in the room. "We are the most powerful beings on this planet. We live forever. We dominate every other species in the world. Human laws don't apply to us anymore."

He sounded a whole lot like their sire, who said shit like that all the time.

Jake could almost hear the same cheers coming from the army that he'd been collecting—the men and women he had convinced to join his ranks.

To take over the world with him and make it a place for vampires to rule it all. Melios's call to arms.

Humans would only be cattle.

Melios's perfect world. No human laws to muck up things.

"Yes, human laws do apply," snapped a woman's voice.

Everyone, Jake included, turned and saw a new woman— a doctor, by the way she dressed—wrap her arm around the nurse, and she guided the woman to the door.

"Who the hell are you to tell me what to do?" Deke growled.

The woman looked like she wanted to scream. And if Jake wasn't mistaken, her face morphed for just a second, elongating, then it stopped.

"I am—"

"I got this, Doc," said another woman as she walked through the door. She had short spikey red hair and dark circles under her eyes. Thin. Short. Sword in hand. Guns strapped to her waist. Body armor.

She might have been considered a cute, petite thing, but her energy was, well, broken or something.

Jake Reynolds had seen a lot of shit. Especially when Melios took him to some weird-assed places he'd never knew existed.

But this gal.

There was something way off about her. Like way, way off.

The woman shoved Travis Collins and Joanie Alekhine into the room. "Here. You lost something, Doc."

Both Collins and Alekhine were bound by what looked to be thin silver chains. And neither one seemed particularly happy about being brought back. Travis had a black eye. Joanie looked like she'd been punched a few times herself.

"You can't do this to us. You can't hold us like prisoners," Alekhine said.

The woman looked at Joanie. "Actually, I can." She waved the sword particularly close to Joanie's face.

Joanie's eyes scraped over the blade, and she stood up straighter.

"Thanks," the doctor said and proceeded to release the chains. The skin looked scorched where the chains had rested on them.

The redhead gave the doctor side-eye, then glanced at the group. She rolled her wrist, making her katana flash in the light, showing exactly how wickedly sharp it was.

She looked at all of them like she was about to start a lecture.

"Is it monologue time?" Malcomb whispered.

Jake shot Malcomb a look.

Malcomb just shrugged.

Pretty sure the redhead with the sword heard it all.

"Now, kids. Here's the deal. You do what I say without question, and we'll all get along just fine."

"Who are you?" Jake asked. "Where's Melios?" He didn't like throwing that out, but in the past, if he and his team ever got into trouble, just bringing up Melios's name was enough to get them out of it.

She raised her eyebrow. "A pile of sooty ash blowing in the wind."

The words slammed into him. While Melios was a fucked-up bastard, he was Jake's sire—Jake's maker. He made every one of them.

Even if the sire was horrible, it was hard to believe that he

26

was actually dead. Melios had been alive for hundreds of years. Nothing should have been able to kill him.

Jake shook his head, trying to wrap his mind around it.

The redhead didn't seem to notice or care. "You vampires are alive at my discretion. You continue to breathe, at my permission."

Deke stepped forward, their differences in size was almost comical. Blood ran down Deke's face, making him look even more the monster.

"You're not the boss of me, little girl."

She turned directly to Deke Smith.

They were separated by a good thirty feet.

Then she disappeared.

What the fuck?

She reappeared directly in front of him, like a phantasm. She was barely corporeal when she pulled up her sword.

And shoved it straight through Deke's chest.

In slow motion, Jake swore he could see each inch of the blade, shining in the bright white of the room as she pulled the sword back.

Then, both slowly, yet still in a blink, Deke Smith disappeared in a puff of ash.

Like a car crash happening.

Both slow and fast.

A special effects movie.

But it was real.

The gray soot that suddenly hung in the room was Deke not a minute before.

Nobody moved.

The dust floated in the air, a horrible haze in the otherwise white room.

What.

The.

Fuck.

She glanced at each one of them in turn. "I'm Eve Harrison. And I will kill any one of you fuckers in a blink because I Do. Not. Care. About any of you. You will do as you're told, or you will die." She took a step away from where Deke had just been standing.

Gray dust covered her.

She didn't bother wiping it off. "Questions?"

"Yeah," Thompson said. "I don't—"

"Shove it up your ass." She glanced around the room, glaring at everyone. "First order of business. Clean this room. You dumb bastards tore it apart. It will be so pristine; I can eat off it. You have one hour. Move."

And with that, Eve Harrison walked out of the room.

The vampires glanced at each other.

"Well, fuck," Malcomb said.

Jake agreed with him.

3

35 MINUTES LATER

*H*e couldn't believe Deke was gone.
Just like that.

Deke Smith was gone.

Would he shed a tear over the bully of a vampire that had sort of made his way into Jake's group? Not likely.

A lot of vampires died. A lot he knew. The more he cleaned, the more the realization came to him. That they were the only survivors. The only ones who made it out.

Fuck.

The kid. What had happened to her? Had she died too? Had they killed a teenage girl also? Were they that cruel?

Did the wolves rip her apart?

He didn't want to think about it. Losing someone in wartime was hard. Unexpected and painful. But usually, it was because someone screwed up.

Deke fucked up. Mouthed off to the wrong person.

Is that what happened to the kid? Had she said something that got her killed too?

Whoever was running this particular company, and whatever they were doing, he didn't know. It didn't feel any different than before. They were just as expendable here as they were for Melios. Or at wartime.

Bodies to fill the hole.

Jake and the others had worked hard to make sure they weren't as expendable to Melios, they still understood the score. If they didn't behave, they died. Plain and simple.

Jake shook his head. Tried to focus on the task.

Pick up the glass. Wipe off counters. Straighten beds.

The damaged equipment was being piled in one corner for disposal, and the rest, they were cleaning and returning to their proper places.

The boys had stripped down out of the hospital robe-shirts which had been stained with all kinds of fluids, including blood, and now they wore just the pants they woke in.

And was it him, or did they all look, well, stronger? Thicker, maybe? Joanie didn't look thicker, but she looked, well, healthier.

They looked like they belonged in a psych ward, all of them in their hospital blue clothing.

His mind kept circling back to what he could remember. The world had shaken him hard in the last half-hour.

Everyone was dead, except the five of them. Melios was killed. And Deke was dead.

Jake wondered if there should have more emotion over Deke's death.

But he didn't.

Deke wasn't a friend. He was a fellow soldier. It should have meant Deke saw things the same as Jake did—a part never leaving the military, not really, all soldiers felt that.

Deke, however, had never seemed to leave the battlefield.

Melios seduced him with promises of power and status. Deke fell for it.

Melios's death hit Jake differently. He didn't witness his

sire's death. He wouldn't consider Melios to be his buddy or any sort of partner, but Melios had been a dependable being in his life for the last decade or so.

Melios must have been a casualty in the battle back at the abandoned building where he had created a residence for himself and his vampires. And of course, anyone he kept there for eating, fucking, or whatever else he felt like doing to them. A house of lust and monsters. Some came and went in dealings with Melios. Others were just food.

The entire experience was starting to feel like a blur, painted over with a strange filter—or maybe reality was just hitting. The time with Melios seemed like something out of a strange dream.

This was reality.

What that meant, though, was yet to be determined. Were they prisoners? Slaves to a new boss that could evidently walk through space and time?

Nothing made hard sense. No concrete answers.

Thinking the kid was gone caused more sadness in him than losing any of the others. The kid, who he'd pretty much watched grow up, always had sort of been around.

And Jake had liked her. They all did. And now even she was gone.

"We're all going out that way," Malcomb said, in the otherwise silent room. "Every one of us will. She'll just pull out that sword and cut us all down, one at a time."

"Probably," Jake said as he straightened the bed he'd been laying on before. Everything in the room had been disrupted in some way or another. A couple of the light fixtures were broken, and glass covered the ground. Joanie swept in one corner, while Travis was attempting to adjust the lights, so they weren't flickering so much.

The place looked like a tornado had gone through.

That weird energy blast thing that Deke did—and he'd

never seen a vampire do that before—had done a lot of damage, outside of the fighting.

Joanie pushed the broom and stared a pile of dirt on the floor. "Uh, guys?"

"What?" Travis asked.

She gestured to the ash, where Deke had been standing. "Do we, uh, sweep it up? What do I do with it?"

Jake didn't know what to say. Melios had tended to ignore any ash that was left after a vampire died. But someone had to clean it up.

Thompson answered. "He's gone. There's no coming back from that. Sweep it up."

Joanie nodded. She inhaled a breath as she did and continued sweeping. Jake watched her for a second. Thompson came over, and helped her, pushing his own broom to clean up the sooty stuff.

Jake shivered as they got it cleaned up. They all were going to wind up just like Deke. Malcomb was absolutely right. Nothing left but the dust on the floor.

Jake focused back on the cleaning at hand. Though really there wasn't much left for him to do. Not by now, anyway. They'd been hustling after the woman left, reorganizing the room, putting everything back in order.

Eve.

Whatever the fuck she was.

The female who took out Deke Smith in a single blow.

Hard to believe anyone could do it. Much less, a female who only came to his shoulder.

"You can't possibly be okay with this," Malcomb said as he pushed a storage shelf back into place.

Jake glanced at Isaac. "We're gathering intel right now. Our best bet is to listen, learn, and find out what our scenario is. What all this is, right now."

Because none of them knew anything about where they were, or what was happening.

"Be good little soldiers for the time being," Thompson added. "Until we can determine the best course."

"Like how to kill our boss," Collins chimed in.

Joanie hit him in the arm. "The room is probably bugged, you idiot."

"So what if it is?" Collins answered. "Knowing how to handle any sort of obstacle is survival, is it not?"

"It is survival, but it might not be wise to discuss it here," Jake said.

Because he'd had the same wonder. How did they kill someone who could disappear right in front of them at any time?

"Don't be a dumbass," Joanie said, shoving him. Then she glanced at Jake. "We're underground. I saw no natural light anywhere, and we got pretty far." She started picking up the scattered IV bags.

Bags filled with blood.

"I just can't get over this," Joanie said, her hand on a blood bag. She sniffed at the bag. "It doesn't smell bad at all. It's not a steak dinner, but it doesn't smell horrible. I totally think I could drink this and be good."

Thompson nodded. "Not what we were told."

Jake glanced at each of them. He hoped they were thinking the same thing he was. "Melios lied about the blood, telling us that blood in bags would not sustain us. That it wasn't fresh enough. If he would lie about a simple thing like that, what else did he lie to us about?"

Footsteps made them all turn.

The woman who'd assisted the nurse earlier was back. The doctor.

Jake looked her up and down. This time, with a more critical eye. He could hear her heartbeat, and the soft pattern sounded slightly faster than it should have—at least for a human. But it wasn't like before, the constant, hard throbbing that no matter what he did, would never just fade into the background.

But he could hear hers. He was sure she had to be mythical, but he wasn't confident what species.

Species? Is that even what to call it?

Whatever. She wasn't the same as Eve Harrison, that much he could tell by scent alone.

"Doctor."

She walked toward him, a bit of a smile on her face, but it didn't reach her eyes. "I am Doctor Criger. I've been overseeing your care since you arrived here."

She brushed her hair out of her face for a moment. The widow's peak on her forehead jumped out at him.

Werewolf.

She was a werewolf.

The ancient enemy of vampires, or so the lore went. And Jake smiled to himself, happy he'd been right she was of mythical origin.

"How is the nurse?" Jake asked.

"He didn't hurt her very badly, did he?" Malcomb asked, from across the room. His fists were clenched when he spoke.

She glanced at Malcomb, then back to Jake. "No, Amy is fine. Thank you for asking. She may have a slight scar, and she's a bit bruised, but she will heal up fine."

"Good," Malcomb said.

"How long have we been here?" Joanie asked.

She glanced at her. "Almost eight weeks." Then she looked around the room. "Thank you for cleaning up."

"We made the mess," Malcomb said.

"Well, the cleaning crews and I appreciate it." She took a few more steps toward Jake. "I'm here to check your vitals."

She had a tablet in under one arm and put the stethoscope in her ear. "Would you mind? On the table please."

Jake climbed onto the table he'd just moved. Then glanced at the others. "Have a seat, guys," he said, over his shoulder. "Doctor here's going to give us all the once-over. Get a clean bill of health."

"You hope," Collins piped up.

And he did.

Because the more Jake Reynolds moved and oriented himself, the better he felt. Almost better than he had in years.

A decade, really.

Joanie hung the last of the bags she'd collected. "If anyone needs a doctor's clearance, it's you, dumbass. I will probably have these scars forever." Joanie shoved Collins, and he caught her and laughed.

"Never said you had to follow me," Collins said.

"Whatever," Joanie answered.

Jake noticed the doctor was taking in the bantering as she tapped a few things on her tablet.

"I'm sorry about your hospital room." He glanced around. "This is a hospital, isn't it?"

"Yes. This part is, anyway." She tapped her device. "What's your name? Your birth name. So, we can match it to public records."

"Jake Reynolds."

"Year of birth?"

"1972."

"Age at your turning?"

"33."

She nodded. "You have any other aliases?"

"Pain in the ass," Malcomb piped up.

"Master Chief," Thompson added.

"Sargent," Joanie also chimed in.

Dr. Criger raised her eyebrow. "So, you're the leader?"

"Highest ranking officer of this group."

She glanced between everyone. "You all still organize by the military?"

"Old habits die hard," Jake replied.

"That could be useful," she said as she put down her tablet.

He wondered what she meant when she touched the metal circle of her stethoscope to his chest—cold as hell against his skin.

He tensed. For a second, anyway. He saw the silver metal and had that moment of anticipation of a silver reaction.

Silver could leave a nice burn mark. He knew from experience.

Mythicals and silver did not go well together.

She paused. "Sorry. I know the steel is cold."

He shook his head. "Wasn't expecting it." Sounded better than admitting he expected a silver burn.

But he should have known better.

She was mythical. She wouldn't have a silver-plated stethoscope.

Would she?

He took a few deep breaths for her, then sat still as she ran her hands over him, feeling his neck, chest, and arms.

While he knew that it was for the exam, he couldn't help savoring the sensation. It had been a very long time since someone touched him gently. And the doc's touch was tender. Soft and delicate.

It soothed him.

He felt connected.

Or maybe that was the fire that was starting to build from the doctor's proximity. Another sensation he hadn't felt in a long time.

Fuck. Thankfully, his pants were loose.

Was he going to have this kind of hardening around every female now?

Her expression remained neutral. He tried to make eye contact with her, but she didn't have it.

She remained focused on what she was doing. Checking him over, in all the boring ways.

She cleared her throat.

For that second, their eyes met.

Did she feel it too? He didn't know.

Instead, she turned and addressed everyone in the room. "I heard you speaking before I came in. Let me make one thing clear to all of you. Blood sustains you. *Any* blood. And you must have it to survive."

She tapped on her tablet again and patted his arm, any bit of connection vanished between the two of them. "You're good."

"That much we know," Jake said.

"Do you now?" There, for a second, her eyes lit with mirth, and the smile she returned glinted with flirtation.

He felt—he didn't know. He looked down, his ears feeling warm. "I meant we knew we needed blood."

"Uh-huh. Is that what it was?"

He met her gaze for a moment. Probably a few moments longer than he should have. There was something so magnetic and intriguing about her eyes.

Something that made him want to take off her doctor's coat and see what was underneath.

"What did you think I meant?" he asked.

She opened her mouth to reply but stopped herself. And did her cheeks get a little bit pink?

Her turn to glanced down.

Malcomb might have smirked from a couple of beds away.

Jake turned and glared at him.

And the moment was lost.

She moved to the next table where Thompson had taken a seat, her cheeks no longer pink, and she was back to business.

"Name," she asked.

"Thompson."

"Full name, please. For records."

He sighed. "Edward Thompson."

"You don't like your name?"

He shook his head. "Let's get on with this."

"You seem rushed," the doctor asked.

"The past is gone. Forward is all that matters."

"Fair enough." And continued with her quick questions.

"Why aren't we hungry?" Thompson asked after she finished. "We were always hungry before."

"We've kept you on a steady diet of blood to keep you all healthy. I don't know how often you fed before, but you must eat about every day or at the least, every other day." She ran her hands over Thompson. "All of you were nearly starved when you were brought in."

Wow.

Because Jake had been lucky if he ate twice a week. They all were. Melios told them they only needed to eat twice a week.

"Are you fucking kidding me?" Malcomb said. "Every day?" Anger seethed through his friend, and Malcomb looked ready to tear the room apart again. Jake didn't disagree with him.

But it wouldn't solve anything.

"Six," Jake said, staring at Malcomb, the nickname referenced their old military ranks.

"Seven," Malcomb snapped back.

The doctor raised her eyebrow.

"If he wasn't already dead, I'd kill him myself," Collins chimed in.

Jake crossed his arms, watching them. Just in case. Because he didn't want any more temper flare-ups.

"But now we know," Thompson said. "We may actually like being vampires now."

The doctor made Thompson jump when she put the stethoscope on his back.

"Good to know your reflexes work." She went through her motions again, her hands running all over his arms.

"You didn't like being vampires?" she asked as she continued her exam.

For some reason, Jake was bothered watching her do it.

Thompson shook his head. "I didn't like being hungry all the time. And there was never enough." He glanced around the room. "Some of us wanted to leave. To try on our own."

"Why didn't you?"

Thompson shrugged. "All for one, and all that, I think."

"I believe you. Werewolves are the same way. For the most part, anyway."

Jake filed that bit in his head—the way she said the last part. It was important. Intimate. And it bothered him that she told it to Thompson.

Could he seriously be jealous of the doctor giving an exam?

What the actual fuck?

"You will all feel, overall, more normal when you're fed. You'll be able to act and walk and be around humans," she said.

"Is that why I can't hear your pulse?" Thompson asked.

"Right. You're fed. I'm sure all of you must have heard that a lot before."

"The pulses? It was constant." Jake added.

She looked at Jake. "Every one of you was half-starved when you were first brought in. It took several bags of blood for each of you to return you to full health. You were always hungry?"

Jake nodded.

"Well, lady and gentlemen, welcome to the real world of being a vampire. You do not have to be hungry every day. As long as you're here in this facility, we'll help you learn what you need to know to survive." She finished with Thompson.

"I am sorry you endured that torture. Mythicals who purposely mislead their flock should be hanged." She spat the last part out like a curse as she walked up to Malcomb's table.

"Preach, sister," Malcomb muttered.

She sort of grinned. But just for a second as she started checking Malcomb over.

"So how much blood do we need?" Joanie asked.

"About a cup a day. Six minutes of feeding time from a donor. However, you don't have to take it all at once from the same donor. You can take a minute or two at a time. Or drink bagged blood whenever you need it."

She did exactly what she did to Jake and Thompson.

"Well, kinda handsy there, aren't you, Doc?" Malcomb asked. "I prefer to at least take you to dinner before you put your hands on me."

Dr. Criger snorted.

Jake gritted his teeth.

"How do you get a donor?" Thompson asked. "Are there people lined up to do this?"

She shook her head. "I don't recommend it. Especially not from a human. If you take too much blood too quickly from a human, you'll make them crazy."

"You mean, literally crazy?" Malcomb asked. "Like unable to determine reality crazy? Or like horny crazy?"

She nodded. "Depending on the situation, yes to both."

Jake met his gaze. Melios had a fetish about making

humans crazed with lust. Many of his flock would feed off humans they brought in. How their responses were controlled, Jake wasn't sure, but many humans were left with strange, drug-like sexual cravings before he'd kill them.

Jake had tried to stay away from the viper pit. They all did.

Maybe that was why they were so starved of food.

"Is there a cure?" Malcomb asked.

She shook her head. "Please don't drink from humans, directly, if you can help it. Save yourself the trouble."

"What about you?" Jake asked. "Could I drink from you?"

"No! Of course not."

"Because you're a werewolf," Jake said.

"Because no werewolf in their right mind would let a vampire drink from them!" She sounded almost appalled that he'd even suggested the scenario.

"Well, that much is true then," Jake said, more to himself than to her.

"What is?"

"The ancient war between vampires and werewolves. That's still a thing."

"Oh, please. No. It isn't." She finished with Malcomb and moved to Collins. "You asked if *you* could drink *my* blood. I said no. It has nothing to do with werewolves versus vampires."

"What does it mean, then?"

"In theory yes, of course, a vampire could drink the blood of a werewolf. I don't know too many werewolves who would allow it."

"So, there's a prejudice," Malcomb said.

She sighed. "Fine. Yes. A bit. While werewolves and vampires are not at war, they aren't friendly. There's some old, ancient passed down bull that some old assed vampire has come up with, but really, the two don't spend a lot of time together. Interspecies mingling is difficult."

"Prejudice?" Collins asked.

She started checking him over. "No. Biology."

"Huh?"

She felt along his arms and shoulders. "Here, at Jackstone Foundation—"

"We're at fucking Jackstone Foundation?" Malcomb asked.

"Yes. Didn't you read all the "Jackstone Foundation" on all the equipment?" she asked as she put her stethoscope on Collins. "Deep breath for me."

Joanie shrugged. "I figured it was donated. Not that it was where we were."

"Surprise," Dr. Criger said, pulling out one arm of the scope as she started checking over Collins.

Collins shook his head. "You do mean the charity corporation? The one that gets kids trips to amusement parks and meets celebrities? That Jackstone Foundation?"

"Yes. That would be the one. Hold your arm up for me."

"Why the hell does Jackstone Foundation have a hospital in the basement for vampires?" Malcomb asked.

She patted Collins shoulder after she finished. "You're good."

She started walking toward Joanie. "Since the owners and founders are vampires."

Thompson barked in a single, hard laugh.

Jake stared at her. "You're kidding."

She shook her head. "James Henrick and Joseph Oliver are vampires. And they run Jackstone with a two-part mission. One part, the upfront public side, is a charity for humans. The backside? That's for mythical issues. Mythicals who need help. Or humans who have been harmed because of mythical activity."

She started checking Joanie over, having her breath in and out for her.

"Humans who have been harmed? Like harmed, how?" Collins asked.

The doctor shrugged as she finished with Joanie. "There's a level of confidentiality involved. I don't know. However, there is one case I worked on I can share with. A human girl was attacked by a werewolf. Scarred pretty badly, both emotionally and physically. The wolf was killed by the Immortal Knights Templar. The girl, who came from an impoverished upbringing, a few years later, was bumped to the front of the line for a few scholarships."

"What happened to her?" Joanie asked.

"She got some scholarships. Not all, but a few. Enough to help with her tuition."

"So how are we connected with that?" Jake asked.

She sighed. "That is up to James Henrick to decide."

Something about the look on her face made Jake pretty darn sure she knew what this James Henrick had in mind for them.

"What about Eve Harrison?" Thompson asked.

She held out her hands. "I assume you all will be told what is expected of you soon."

"So, something is expected of us," Malcomb said.

She nodded. "No one gets anything for free at Jackstone. There's always a price."

That, Jake believed.

4

"*A*ll of you probably want some real clothing," Megan Criger said to the room of vampires as she sat a pile of sweatpants and sweatshirts on a nearby bed.

Especially since the boys were naked.

From the waist up.

She couldn't help staring, because these guys were undoubtedly—

In. Shape.

By the stars, she'd never been attracted to vampires before. She'd always sort of considered them beneath her. Of course, all the ones she'd ever really been around were practically the mythical version of crack heads. When she met them, they were usually having some kind of blood overdosing issue.

Most vampires were addictive-type personalities who thought they were better than everyone else. Ego and addiction were not a great combination.

She expected the disaster that had followed when they woke. She'd assumed they'd go bonkers and rip apart the hospital—exactly why she had them put in this corner, where no one else was. Just in case.

But that was the first few minutes.

Just interacting with them now though, she could tell, even from the way they spoke, they weren't like others she had been around.

Isaac Malcomb flexed his arm. "What, our beefy bicep too much for you, Doc?"

"Knock it off, Malcomb," Jake Reynolds said. "Your muscles aren't that impressive."

I wouldn't say that she thought to herself. They all were impressive.

"Oh, lord, here they go," Joanie said. "Now, Doc, they're going to impress you."

She glanced at her. "Try. They'll try to impress me." And winked.

"Oh, no, now we can't have that," Travis Collins said.

"You're so funny, with your attempts," Edward Thompson said. And as the largest of the remaining ones, he was a sight to behold.

And off they all went. Flexing muscles.

Playing.

They were playing.

It made her laugh. She never saw vampires acting like this. Like boys. Not mythical crackheads.

Joanie laughed too. "Get over it, you dorks. I'm sure the Doc sees better every day."

She blushed. She wouldn't mind having a bunch of men—even if they were vampires—strutting around her house to amuse her with their muscled bodies.

"Vampires, not really," she finally said. "But again, I don't mingle with too many."

"Do you need some vampires to mingle with, Doc?" Malcomb asked.

"Thank you, no." She shook her head, focusing on why she was there and started sorting the clothing by sizes. "I have various sizes of clothes for you to choose from." It gave her fingers, and her mind something to do, so she wasn't ogling the men.

And regardless she was a doctor, and she had a clinical duty to care for these mythicals, she could not get over how hot the men looked in their hospital pants, hung low on their very toned hips.

Broad chests, every one of them.

Cool skin.

Examining them all was hard...

Especially Mister Jake Reynolds.

Megan's gaze would dart over to him. He was the one she'd look at, when she'd be alone in the wing, watching the patients.

Why she wasn't sure. But she couldn't help herself.

Maybe it was because she was a sucker for that dusty blond hair he had. Long, scruffy, but still had that glint in the light—

"I thought we were at the height of fashion in these soft pants," Malcomb said, drawing her out of her wandering mind.

She glanced at the vampire. "Mister Malcomb," Megan said, smiling just a bit. "You have been asleep for eight weeks. Not eight decades. Fashion has not changed that much."

He snapped his fingers. "Well, shit. These are quite comfortable."

A couple of the other vampires smirked.

"Knock it off, Malcomb," Reynolds said. "Don't befuddle the doctor."

"'Befuddle?' What the fuck? Are you eighty now?" Collins asked.

Reynolds sighed. "I still have manners." He ran his hands through his hair, and down over his bit of a beard.

They all had beards—sort of. Not full-grown sexy beards, but "getting there" stubble from the weeks in the coma. Just enough to be there, but not enough to be full beards.

She couldn't wait to see him shaved.

If he shaved.

Of course, he did. And then she'd be able to see the jawline hidden under his beard.

Stop it.

Behave. He's a damned bloodsucker. And a patient.

Regardless, he was pretty to look at.

Even when he picked up a gray sweatshirt and slipped it on, he was still handsome. The others did the same, selecting shirts and extra sweatpants.

"We have clothes, thanks," Reynolds said. "We can get them from the building downtown. Assuming we're still in Liverly?"

She nodded. "You are still in Liverly, yes. I don't know about your possessions. The building burned to the ground."

"What?" Each one of them voiced outcry or anger at the news.

"What are we—"

"Now, where do we go?"

"Where am I supposed to go now?"

"This is so screwed up!"

"What kind of messed up bullshit is this?"

They were more upset over this than they were about the news of their master's death. Of course, from what Megan had gleaned about this Melios guy, she shouldn't be surprised.

She sighed. "Please. Calm down."

It wasn't working.

She gritted her teeth. Inhaled a breath, ready to—

"Attention!" Though it sounded like "Atten-Hut!" to her, every one of the vampires stopped what they were doing and stood straight and tall. They sort of got in a line as well.

Jake glanced back at her. "You have the floor, doctor."

She nodded.

"Thank you." She pursed her lips together. "Look, I don't know the circumstances, except that your, uh, nest, was burned. If there was any property found, I'm not aware of it."

"What do we do about clothing? Weapons? Shoes?" Joanie asked. "Personal effects?"

"A place to live. We'll need a place to live," Malcomb said, giving Joanie some serious side-eye.

"Here," snapped a voice from the door.

Megan glanced to the door. The sheldevak James had hired to control these vampires was back.

Eve Harrison.

Lovely.

Was she going to slay more of them?

What in the world was Henrick thinking, bringing her in here? Megan thought a sheldevak would be the last resort, in case the vampires went crazy or something and had to be eliminated.

Not brought in as their leader.

She took a couple of steps toward Eve, but not because she wanted to be friendly, or show solidarity.

"Where? In this hospital room?" Malcomb asked.

"You'll live in the barracks," Eve said.

"There's barracks? Like military barracks?" Thompson asked.

"No, there's not," Megan interjected. "Not exactly."

"Oh, doctor, if you know everything, then by all means, please," Eve Harrison said. She grabbed a nearby chair, spun it and straddled it, elbows on the back, eyes wide like she mimicked a child. "Because I want to know why the fuck I'm here."

A couple of the vampires smirked.

Megan growled. Deep in her chest, the growl rumbled, the beast daring to be let free. It always wanted to leap free when she was stressed or threatened.

Right now, even though Harrison was sitting in a chair, she certainly felt like a threat.

And the beast wanted to rip through the sheldevak.

"I merely meant, that no, we do not have military barracks here. We do, however, have an area with temporary housing until a more permanent solution is available." She glared at Eve.

Eve rolled her eyes. "So, barracks."

"Barracks typically mean one room and rows of beds. This is more of a dormitory."

"Whatever," Eve said, and she stood up again. "Bottom line, you all have beds. Not in this room. Let's move on because I'm not about to dwell on trivial bullshit." She glared at Megan. "Right, Doc?"

"Sure," Megan said. Out of habit, she glanced at her tablet. Data scrolled on the screen, from the floor above.

She needed to go make her rounds. She started to head on her way.

"Leaving us, Doc?" Thompson asked.

"I have rounds," she said as she walked toward the door.

She made it outside and glanced back in.

Just to make sure Eve Harrison wasn't slaughtering them all.

Jake's gaze was on Eve Harrison. "What is this about, sir?"

Eve put her hands on her hips. "Congratulations. You are now the property of Jackstone Foundation, as part of their ongoing mission of working with mythicals needs. You will do as you're told when you're told to do it. There will be no questions asked. If you are told to protect a mythical, then you will provide the necessary security. If you are told to keep a human out of harm's way, you will do everything in your power to fulfill that."

She walked around the room, her gaze moving over each one of them.

"What if we don't want to?" Collins asked.

Megan froze.

Would she do it again? Take out another one of these vampires before he'd even gotten an assignment?

Eve raised an eyebrow and took a couple of steps toward Collins. "If you want to keep walking the world, you'll do as you're told."

She didn't pull out a sword.

Progress, maybe?

MEGAN WALKED through the hospital wing and found Amy at the nurse's station.

"What are you doing here?" She put her hand on her hip. "I specifically remember telling you to go home. Get some rest."

Amy shrugged. "Home would be boring. I'd just lay around and freak myself out. At least here, I can get things done." She put her hand on her neck. "And here, I get sympathy attention. Besides, par for the course. Mythicals can be primal beasts coming out of any sort of coma or anesthesia. I should have been paying more attention to his vitals."

Megan nodded. "Yes, probably should have. Bet you don't do that again."

"Probably not," Amy said.

Megan looked in her eyes and casually checked her over.

The bandage was clean, so her wound wasn't seeping anymore.

Good.

Her color was starting to come back. But the dark circles under her eyes were still there. She didn't look right yet.

She raised an eyebrow. "You didn't drink your tea, did you?"

"I did drink a little," she said, pulling away. "Fairy Tea makes me jittery. And I don't like it."

"Come here," Megan said, motioning her into an empty room. This wasn't like Amy at all. "What's going on?"

"I'm fine," Amy said, crossing her arms.

And she winced.

"Uh-huh. Let me see."

Amy raised her shirt. Her ribs were bruised in several places. "What in the world?" Megan gritted her teeth as she put her hands on her ribs. "What did that vampire do to you?"

"I'll be fine," Amy said. "I'll just drink some more tea."

Megan tried to remember—did that vampire have her in some kind of vice grip to hurt her ribs? It all happened so fast, she couldn't remember exactly. Just that he'd had a hold of Amy and bit her.

"This needs more than tea. It needs to be set."

"Really, I'm fine," Amy said. "It's nothing."

"It's not nothing," Megan said. "Stay here. Let me get something to set that with."

She stepped back out in the hall, shaking her head.

The damned woman had so much pride. Would never admit to being hurt.

Why didn't she say something?

Megan stepped up to the controlled substances room and put her hand on the scanner. When it released the door, she headed in and went to the back wall of magical potions and treatments.

Just like in a human hospital, some treatments were kept under security to prevent theft and abuse.

Full strength Fairy Tea and treatments from Avalon were kept secure, and to be used as needed. Not all cases required treatment from magical devices.

Mythicals, like herself, who were human most of the time, responded traditionally to human-based medicines. Others, like Amy or the vampires, responded to medications based on their origins. Most vampire meds tended to be blood-based. Amy responded best to Avalon-based healing techniques.

Like Fairy Tea.

Or Avalonian seaweed wraps.

Megan entered her passcode and quantity request on the display where the seaweed was stored. It opened, revealing two strands of the plant. She grabbed them and headed back to Amy.

"Oh, you did not," Amy said, rolling her eyes.

"I did," she said, holding up the seaweed wraps. "Why are you so against anything from Avalon?"

"I just don't think all that is necessary. It's bruised ribs. I'll be fine. Swear."

"If you were going to be fine, you'd be looking a lot better than you are right now," Megan said. She gestured for her to raise her arms.

"A patient can refuse treatment," Amy said as she held her arms up.

Megan applied the two strips to help the wounds head. "I won't force you to drink more tea, but I *highly suggest* you have another cup of Fairy Tea and have another one when you get home, to help you heal faster."

Amy sighed. "I will do it. Under protest."

"Good," Megan said.

"How are they? The others?" Amy asked as she hopped off the exam bed. With a lot less gusto as she usually had.

Megan watched her favoring her side.

"And you don't need treatment," she muttered.

"I'll be fine," Amy replied. "Now, you didn't answer my question."

She waved her hand. "They are fine. I am going to go down and run more tests on them later after they get settled into their dormitory."

She grimaced. "Great. I'll have neighbors."

"It's only temporary," Megan said. "Henrick told me he was working on a permanent facility for them off-site."

"You know, when I was hired here, it was supposed to be a temporary housing on the property. But look who's still living in the basement among other wandering mythicals."

"Maybe it's time you looked for a new place, too."

She shrugged. "Maybe. Stars know I don't want to live next to someone who could decide to have a midnight snack and eat me."

Megan couldn't help smirking. "I get that."

5

*J*ake Reynolds glanced around the dormitory. It wasn't like any dorm he'd ever stayed in. An apartment, practically. Not like the bed lined, one-room barracks he'd expected to find.

"Two of you will need to bunk up," Jake said, glancing between everyone. There were only four bedrooms and five of them.

And one of them was a female, so Joanie got her own room.

"Fuck," Malcomb said. "And how are we going to figure that?"

"Rank."

"Well, what about me? I'm not military," Collins said.

"Aww, it's cute you want to use your former military ranks to create order," Eve Harrison said.

Reynolds glared at her.

She just grinned. "Listen, kids. Figure it out. Any infighting will be dealt with." Something drew her attention. "Immediately," she said, heading toward the front door.

A tall man in a suit stood there, and he gestured for Eve.

She glanced back at the group. "Get sorted. We've got work to do."

Jake nodded. "We got this."

After Eve walked away, Joanie came out of the master bedroom. "I'll just take this master suite," Joanie said, clutching her bundle of sweats she'd gotten in her arms.

Jake glanced at her. He was about to object. As the ranking officer, the leader, he'd figured he'd get first pick.

But Joanie was a girl. And needed a bit more privacy. More than she'd ever gotten at Melios's nest, anyway. Worry wormed its way through his gut, probably the only emotion he'd really felt before, but now, it was stronger. More genuine.

He'd done his best, he and the rest of them, to protect her, and give her some semblance of dignity in that monster's pit. Even under whatever the fuck they were under before, they had some respect for Joanie.

Every memory he had of what he'd witnessed and endured, all at the entertainment of Melios, made his stomach ill. A lot of shit went down in that nest.

Damn.

Now is not the time for this.

His gaze hit Joanie again. "Yeah. Good," Reynolds said, returning to the moment. "You take the master with your own bathroom."

She almost squealed.

Almost.

"The rest of us share these two bathrooms," Reynolds said. "The biggest room has bunks. The other two have single beds." He glanced at a room next to Joanie's, the one that sort of buffered her from everyone else. "I'll be here."

Thompson stuck his head in the room with the bunk beds. "Collins and I'll take the bunks."

"Guess that means I'm here," Malcomb said, gesturing to the last remaining room.

Jake nodded. "Put your shit down. Be ready in five."

"Sir, yes, sir."

They were settled quickly, and they all took a seat in the living area.

Waiting.

Jake Reynolds didn't intend to eavesdrop, but Eve Harrison was just outside the door, yelling.

"You're crazy James," Eve Harrison said, glaring at another man—vampire by the look of him, just outside the dormitory door. Same light-colored eyes all vampires seemed to have.

"You're what they need, Eve."

"No, I am fucking am not," she snarled back. "I'm not what anyone needs. You fucking know that. I can't play nicey-nicey after the last couple of months. I won't."

"I didn't ask you to. And I don't want you to. I want you to be mean. I want you to push them. And I want you to take out whoever doesn't make the cut." He glanced in the room and then back at her. "Like you already have. I want you to be you. Not some sweet version of it."

She snorted.

Reynolds raised his eyebrow and glanced at Malcomb.

Malcomb nodded.

Evidently, their fearless leader hadn't had the best last few months. That could prove interesting intel. He made another note—never knew when it would come in handy.

"I know it's sucked. I get it. I do. You need this, Eve. As much as they need it." James rubbed his head. "Give them six months. If they don't turn into upstanding mythicals, then take them out."

She nodded. "I don't get why you're doing this."

"Debts have to be paid."

Jake glanced up just in time to see Eve Harrison tip her head to the side. "Who are you paying, James?"

He hesitated for a second. "I appreciate you doing this."

She put her hands on her hips. "I expect to be paid. Especially with all the changes I have to make for you—"

"You will. As discussed." He glanced into the dormitory. Right at Jake. "Now, let's find out if they're going to work."

"You crazy bastard," Eve muttered as they came inside.

Everyone had sort of gathered in the living room.

She glanced around. "Alrighty, kids. Here's what's up. Long story short, this is James Henrick. He fucking owns your ass. You do whatever the fuck he tells me to have you do. It's probably going to involve a fair amount of ass-kicking. If that's a problem with any of you," her gaze landed right on Jake.

Which pretty much pissed him off.

"I need to know right now," Eve finished, looking at everyone else.

No one moved.

She glanced at the other man. "James, you're up. Tell the wonderful kids what they won."

James gave Eve some side-eye, then smiled and looked at the rest of them. "For the next six months or so, you will be part of Jackstone Foundation. A Cold Team."

"A what?" Jake asked.

"A Cold Team. One of our special security teams."

"This is a security job?" Malcomb grumbled. "I wanted ass-kicking."

James smiled. "It's security. And I cannot promise ass-kicking, but mythicals, as a general rule, tend to fight, so there's a good chance in every scenario, there will be some ass-kicking. Again, the work is classified as security. You'll be protecting those who have been harmed and/or are in danger of being attacked by mythicals. Essentially, you'll be an arm of the Immortal Knights Templar."

Jake shook his head. Melios had a lot of things to say about the Immortal Knights Templar. Not nice things, either. How they meddled in affairs and caused general problems in the mythical community.

Hell, Jake followed one of them for a while, then had to report back. And the Knight always imposed his will on others with very little consideration. Mythicals died because of the Templars.

Every day.

At the time, he'd never considered Melios could be wrong about the Templars. Of course, at the time, he believed everything he'd been told.

Now, however, he questioned what he knew. After all, his sire lied about the blood.

"Aren't the Templars bad guys?" Collins asked. "That's what we'd always been told."

"Consider the source," she said. "Your sire thought humans should be meat, and vampires should rule the world."

Melios had taken a great deal of time, making sure they all understood his vision of their place in the world. That's what they all had been taught, from day one. Humans were cattle. And they were the farmers.

And Melios was the king.

And it made sense.

It entirely made sense to them.

Waking up here, perhaps because he wasn't starving, Jake didn't feel the oppressive influence which had overrun him for almost a decade.

It was almost like being alive again.

Deke, however, had still believed in Melios's teachings.

Jake woke and felt almost normal. Deke woke and felt power.

While they hadn't been given time to find out if Deke would have changed his thinking, Jake doubted that Deke would have ever felt like a human.

He believed too much in what Melios had been saying.

"We all believed him," Thompson said. "Melios, I mean."

James nodded, with sympathy in his eyes. "You were committed to him. He was your master. Your sire. He made you. And in essence, hypnotized you into believing him. Melios was a very old and powerful vampire. We don't know how he put such a hold on you, but we know his talent for mental manipulation was far beyond most vampire skills."

"You seem to know a lot about this," Joanie said.

James met her gaze. "His methods are not unknown to me."

"Get over it," Eve said, her gaze darting to James and back to the others. "He's dead. You're not. End of file."

"That's cold," Thompson said.

"Grow up. I got no time for emotional babies," Eve countered.

Thompson looked like he was going to retort, but Jake shot him a look.

Thompson chilled.

James glanced at Eve for a moment, then back at the others. "Dr. Criger will be checking in regularly, to make sure all of you are now under your own cognitive control."

Cool, Jake thought.

"Oh, we're under our own power. Buzzing's gone." Joanie put it perfectly into words. The buzzing in the back of their heads had vanished.

"It makes what I need from you easier, and what the Templar Knights need, simpler to understand."

"What exactly do they do?" Jake asked.

"The Templars protect humans from mythicals and protect mythicals from being discovered by humans. They are a bridge between humans and mythicals. But there's only so many of them. Here at Jackstone, we attempt to assist them in any way they need. Hence, you."

"What do you mean? Are we new? Or is this something you've done before."

"Your military and police backgrounds from your human lives make you ideal for this. I am hoping, through re-education and training, that you will make a great addition to our teams of mythicals."

"And if we don't?" Joanie asked.

"You'll die," James replied.

6

LATER THAT NIGHT

*D*ark. Swirling dark.
    Anger.
Fear.
Hunger.
So much hunger.
Fighting. Attacking. Surrounding him. Destroying him.
"No, wait," Megan cried. "He's just hungry!"
But the metal flew.
And his head was sliced off.
It hit the ground with a hard bounce, landing at her feet.
The open eyes stared at her. The fangs bared, blood coating them.
Jake Reynolds.
He disappeared into a pile of soot and ash.

MEGAN BOLTED UP, gasping for air. The images of the dream filled her head.

Her hand to her chest, she couldn't breathe for a second.

She glanced around. She was home, in her bedroom. In

the small, two-bedroom cottage she bought last year. It was close to downtown and Jackstone, but far enough away, it wasn't consumed by the late-night traffic.

And there wasn't an attack.

No one was being killed.

No heads on the ground. Or ash.

She shook her head. It had to be residual from the eventful day. She tugged at the gown that felt stuck to her.

She patted her forehead and felt the moisture there.

Sweat. Great.

Well, that's what late summer did in the Midwest. It got hot and sweaty at night. Her phone sat on the floor next to the bed, the notification light blinking.

Of course, it was.

She leaned down and grabbed it from its charger and looked to see if the notification was anything important. Like work.

Or if it was another email from that shopping website where she spent all her money.

Yep. Shopping. Nothing important. Just another lightning deal she should buy. Because she needed another pair of shoes.

The streetlight outside cast just enough light, she could make out the wall of shoes in the corner.

No, she didn't need a new pair of mules. She had seven pair.

She ran her hand over her head again and felt her sweat-soaked hair. Yeah, it wasn't just a cute little mini bit of moisture on her brow. This was middle-of-the-night-shower-level sweat.

She climbed out of bed. When she moved the sheets, she could feel that they were damp too.

"Good grief," she muttered. "I know it's hot, but sheesh," she said as she started stripping the sheets.

"Because I wanted to remake my bed in the middle of the night," she said when she got out a fresh set of sheets. She still felt gross, though. And under her skin, she felt her beast clawing at her.

Like the monster wanted to run.

Hard.

She threw the bedding down and headed into her back yard.

Bones popped. Hair grew. Things stretched.

She had only moments left where she still had control.

Just around the block.

Just—

Then all at once, Megan was on all-fours, the werewolf was in charge. What she wanted no longer mattered.

The wolf ran in circles, the well-worn path marking where the wolf had done this before, many times.

Circle.

Circle.

Circle.

Leap.

And bam.

The wolf was free. Outside, and able to run.

The wolf, being in charge, ran. She ran up and down Liverly's streets. Through fields, and into neighborhoods. Dogs barked. Cats hissed.

Wolf didn't care.

Wolf ran.

Anything to get away from the nightmare.

WOLF STOP.

She took a deep breath.

Prey in the area. Two more deep sniffs. Forward. Move careful. Stalk the prey.

The wolf moved around the corner. The tall rocks —*buildings*—came from some other part. Something that recognized the surroundings.

Wolf didn't care.

Wolf wanted to find the prey.

Ground changed.

Grass now hard.

Forward. Into the cave with its angular lines.

Garage.

Shadows all around. Wolf walked careful. Following scent.

Through the hard cave.

There. In the shadows. Just in the moonlight. Wolf's eternal enemy. Prey. Must be destroyed. The wolf charged.

The shadow turned.

"Hey, dog."

The wolf froze.

Growled.

The prey tipped his head.

No fear in him. None. Wolf always smelled fear. Prey had none. Wolf bared teeth.

Prey held out upper paw. *Hand.* Wolf closed in. Sniffed.

And the smell was known to the wolf. Not wolf. To the other place. Wolf jumped back. This was not just any prey.

I know this...

Wolf growled again, but softer. Stepped closer to prey. Sniffed.

Prey opened hand. "Good dog." Prey rubbed muzzle.

Wolf stepped in closer. Prey stroked head.

"You're a big boy, aren't you?" Prey said.

Wolf groaned.

"Hang with me. We can watch the stars," Prey said.

Wolf followed Prey to a wall. Wolf put paws up to see.

"Big world out there," Prey said. "And it's getting more and more complicated by the minute."

Prey pet wolf again.

"Got a name?" he asked.

Wolf growled.

He smirked. "I'm Jake. Jake Reynolds. And evidently, I'm still a vampire."

The words meant something to the wolf. A lot of something. But not to Wolf. To the other side.

Jake...

Wolf bumped Jake Prey.

Jake Prey patted his chest. "Come on. Let's see what we can find you to eat."

Hungry. Food. Yes.

Wolf trotted after Jake Prey.

7

"What the hell is that thing?" Joanie asked Jake.

He glanced down at his new friend who happily chewed on the huge bone Jake had found in a storage closet. "Dog."

"Jake, that is not a dog. That's a friggin' wolf."

Jake looked back at the animal and shrugged. "Wolf. Dog. Whatever."

The wolf growled.

Jake patted it's back. "Shh, easy."

The wolf growled again.

Jake glanced in the wolf's eyes. "Easy. No one here's gonna hurt you." He petted the muzzle again.

The wolf made a whimper-type sound.

"You do know, the last time we were around some of these things, they were trying to kill us," Joanie said.

Jake nodded. "You can't be sure this is a werewolf."

She raised her eyebrow. "Really? It's a wolf. In downtown. A large wolf. I'd bet that thing weighs one-hundred thirty pounds, easy. That's one thing that Melios taught us. They're bigger than a regular wolf or large dog. It's a damn werewolf."

Jake remembered the lesson. One of the few that Melios actually bothered giving them about the mythicals in the world. "Something about mass can't disappear, only reorganize or some such."

Joanie nodded. "Right. A two-hundred-pound man made a two-hundred-pound wolf."

He raised his eyebrow. "I wonder if there are exceptions to the rule?"

Joanie shrugged. "Probably. There's always something." She kept her distance from the wolf. "Still doesn't explain why you brought a wolf in here."

"Hungry."

"It's 3 in the morning."

He sighed. "I've done enough sleeping for a while. I couldn't rest anymore."

She nodded and sighed. "I think all of us have been up. Malcomb and Thompson are sparring in the humongous gym. Did you see it? It's like massive. Mats and everything."

He smiled. "Better than the dark, dank basement?"

"Oh yeah," Joanie said. "I was in there for a while. Practicing. Moving. We all were feeling restless. Well, all but Travis. He, however, can sleep through the end of the world."

Jake smirked. Travis was always able to sleep.

"What's keeping you up, Oh Glorious Leader?" Joanie asked and pulled a bag of blood out of the fridge. Eve had shown up with a box of bagged blood and put them all in the fridge, so they had food to eat when they were hungry.

Though Jake would love a steak. He needed to look into that. Could he have steak? He figured he'd ask Dr. Criger the next time he had a chance. She would know, he imagined.

The wolf paused, sniffed, and went back to chewing the bone Jake had found.

He smirked at the nickname. And patted the wolf's head again. "Everything. It seems like yesterday we were ripping apart werewolves and fighting men with swords. Guess they were Templars, weren't they?

"Probably," Joanie replied.

"I keep thinking about the whole thing. The orders we followed." His hand went down and petted the wolf's head. The wolf paused long enough to lean into the movement before returning to the bone.

"Yeah? What about them?"

"Weren't we all just following orders?"

"So? That's what we do."

He shook his head. "Here's the thing, though. We didn't have all the information. We didn't know what we needed to survive."

"And your point?"

"Maybe they didn't either. The wolves. They just fought us. Because that's what they were told to do. We did the same. Because we were told." He shook his head. "I don't want to go back to living like that."

She raised her eyebrow. "You do know that's a problem when you're any kind of soldier, right? No one ever tells the grunts the whole story."

"That's my point." Jake felt it in his heart. "We need to know. From now on."

"Good luck with that," Joanie said.

The wolf yawned.

Stood.

Groan-growled at Jake.

And turned around and walked out.

Jake glanced at Joanie. "I'll think of something." He turned to the wolf. "Ready to go?" Jake said.

The noise that came out of the wolf was as close to affirmative as Jake had ever heard from an animal.

"Well, I'll show you the door."

But the wolf took off like it knew where it was going.

He turned to follow the animal. Just in case it couldn't open any doors.

But he had a feeling the animal knew where it was going better than he did.

8

ow, this...
        This, we know.

Reynolds darted left as Malcomb took a swing.

Back and forth they went, round and round on the thick mats. High ceilings made it feel like an updated high school gym, not a basement under a building.

Much better than sparring in a dark alley anyway. It had been a while—not just because of the two-month coma-thing they were in, either.

Coach Eve was right there, too. "Harder. Push harder."

Malcomb glared back at Eve Harrison. "I don't want to kill him." He glanced back at Jake and grinned. "Today."

"Fuck that," Eve replied. "You can't kill him."

"Oh, I bet I could," Malcomb replied.

Jake stepped into Malcomb's space. "You wanna try?"

"Get over it, you idiots. Didn't you read your books?"

After getting settled into their apartment, Eve had brought them each a bound textbook-like manual that read like a history of the world, from the mythical point of view.

The Abridged Balance Mandate.

Rules. History. Strengths. Weaknesses. Even family trees and general knowledge.

And it seemed that everything was in there. A primer for being a vampire. Or any other type of mythical.

And fuck there were a lot of them.

"Yeah," Jake replied.

"It's right there in the book. Some fucking divine joke— you cannot kill the same species you are. You all could go full-on fighting in the gym, but you couldn't kill each other. I, however, can kill every one of you, because I'm not a vampire."

"So you've demonstrated," Jake said.

The tension crackled between them all for a few seconds.

She glared at him, her eyes like hard rocks—no emotion in them at all, that he could see.

He still hadn't gotten to anything about her species —sheldevak.

She put her hands on her hips. "Don't hold back. Fight hard. You need the practice."

Jake gritted his teeth and felt his teeth elongating.

Malcomb grinned. His own teeth were longer as well. "This could be fun."

"Ready?"

"Oh yeah, Master Chief."

Jake raised his eyebrow, and off they went.

Harder.

Faster.

And no holding back. It was sort of freeing, knowing that they wouldn't actually kill each other.

Hurt each other? Sure.

But kill?

It was a helpful safety net. Silver lining and all that.

So much to learn. But Jake was working on it. They all were. They'd been so mind-fucked, it seemed the more they learned, the less of what they knew actually wound up being true.

Eve started them on the chapters about vampires and the vampire clans. It went into detail about the difference between a nest of vampires—like what they were with Melios—and a family, which were born vampires, born to breeding vampires.

That was another thing—vampires could actually have children. Jake had always thought they could only bite people, and sire offspring, but no, there were genetically born vampires, with family and siblings, and all that.

It seemed the more Jake read, the more he realized how much Melios had fucked with them all to keep them compliant. The crap he fed them about the way of the world seemed so far away from what it really was.

Jake wanted to understand what he was and how he fit into the world now. Beyond being a Cold Team for Jackstone.

A strange sound made him glance over his shoulder. Two men, large and thick, came into the gym. They moved fast and growled a lot.

"Oh, look. New recruits," one said.

Malcomb broke the sparring. "And you would be? Resident growlers?"

Their smell was distinct—werewolf.

Jake was getting used to it. The wolf he'd met outside that first night had been back. He'd hang with the animal, have a snack, and he'd talk about what he'd learned.

The wolf was a good listener and intelligent behind the eyes.

Similar to these two who just rolled up on them. Similar, but not the same.

One snorted. The other, ironically, growled. They came toward Reynolds and Malcomb.

"What you got in there, vamp?" The second man puffed his chest out. "Wanna go a few?"

"Any time, any place," Malcomb said.

"You have no idea what you've asked for." The second man pushed Malcomb.

Malcomb shoved back.

The less-friendly man struck Malcomb around the middle and slammed him into the ground.

"Enough!"

Everyone froze.

Eve Harrison came over. "Aikers! Johansen! Get the fuck out of here before I turn you into minced meat."

Both men jumped. Johansen, who'd shoved down Malcomb, snarled again and looked like he was going to spit on Malcomb.

Malcomb leaped up—and actually got a little air when he did it—ready to fight.

And in a flash, Eve reappeared next to Johansen. A sharp blade against the man's throat. "Every beast dies when their head pops off."

"I'm not afraid of you, girl," Johansen snapped.

Reynolds took a breath. And the nastiest smell hit him.

What the hell was that?

It wasn't bodily, at least not that he'd ever smelled.

Eve inhaled a big, exaggerated breath. "I beg to differ, but I smell otherwise."

She glanced at Reynolds and Malcomb. "Smell that, boys? That's fear. Every being on this planet gives off this scent when they're afraid. Your wonderful vampire senses will pick it up super easily." She let go of Johansen. "Thanks for the teaching moment, boys. Now get the fuck out of here."

"Fuck you, Eve."

Aikens gestured for Johansen to move along.

"Not on your best day, Johansen," she said as she walked away.

"Wouldn't want to," he snarled back. "Not something that old."

Eve spun and threw her blade. Pierced his shoulder.

"Fuck!" Aikens reached up and pulled it out of Johansen's shoulder.

"Good God, Eve. Really? He has a mission later." The guy flung the blade back but didn't get the distance Eve had, and it hit the floor right in front of her.

"He should know better than to fuck with anything that's mine."

"Eve!"

"Go drink some tea. He'll be fine. It's a flesh wound." The knife was covered in blood, all the way to the hilt, and she picked it up, wiped it on her leg.

Jake stared at her.

"Did you want a taste?" she asked.

Jake shook his head. "I'm interested in your definition of a flesh wound. Because that didn't look like the blood of a flesh wound."

She raised her eyebrow. "You still got a lot to learn, boy."

Just about then, James Henrick, the CEO guy, came over —he'd been sparring with Thompson—and glanced at Eve, then at the other two, then back at Eve.

"Problem?"

"Your wolves are assholes."

Jake looked back at them. He hoped neither one of those assholes were who he was spilling his guts to every night. Though if they were, Jake had a feeling they would have said something. Jake would have were the situation reversed.

"They're my best Cold Team," Henrick said.

Eve glared at him. "Right now."

He sighed. "You seriously think you can turn these

ignorant vampires into an effective team? Not just any team, but my best Cold Team?"

Her gaze darted to Jake, Malcomb, and then across the room to the others. Everyone had stopped and was listening to the exchange.

And Jake was pretty sure he did not like the boss anymore.

He kinda wanted to show the arrogant fucker just how ignorant he was.

Eve didn't have it, either. "I can do anything I fucking want to."

Henrick raised an eyebrow.

"And right now," she said, her gaze running over the team, and back. "Right now, I will make them into the best damn team you got."

"Yeah," Jake said. "The best."

He and Eve exchanged glances.

Whether he liked it or not, she was growing on him.

Sort of.

She clapped her hands. "Okay, everyone, back to sparring. We got a lot to learn and no time to learn it all. You guys need to be dropping your opponents in three to five moves. That's it. You won't have time for more."

And on went the lessons.

9

*M*egan sighed. She didn't like that she had to make the reservation she was about to make. After a long day in the hospital, this was the last thing she wanted to do.

But what choice did she have? She was a werewolf, after all. Certain arrangements had to be made.

She pulled out her phone and typed up the text message that reminded her exactly which part of her was in charge.

The beast.

Sometimes, it felt like the beast was always in charge. No matter what she wanted to do. The last few nights, it was all she could stand to let the wolf run because if she didn't, the damn thing would make her miserable.

Whatever the wolf did on her runs, though, she woke almost every day, wanting to scream about eating prey.

She just hoped the wolf wasn't out eating family pets. And whether she liked it or not though, the beast was running hot for a certain vampire.

Or maybe that was her, and she was using the beast as an excuse.

Megan would have thought, just avoiding the vampires in the basement—how did that not sound like a cheesy horror movie—would have lessened the weird feelings she was having for her patient.

Something she never, ever had.

She finished her text message.

Confirming my reservation for a room. Dr. Megan Criger.

It only took a few moments before her phone lit up with a reply.

Reservation confirmed. Dr. Megan Criger. One room. Double locks.

Megan nodded. Some people thought her reserving a room in the Underground a bit over the top when she could probably have a pen installed in her home, but that would have to be explained later if she sold the place.

Cages weren't exactly fashionable anymore.

She tucked the phone away and felt her little tablet in her bag, so she could check on all the little bloodsuckers. See how they were assimilating to their new apartment.

Going down to see the vampires at the end of her shift meant they should just be waking up or getting around or something since it was just after dusk.

At least, she assumed they were on a typical vampire sleep schedule.

They hadn't left the basement yet.

She stepped into the elevator to take her down. The gray doors were almost closed when she saw a flash of pink and the familiar smell of a day of hell in the hospital.

Yes, Megan knew that smell quite well.

She hit the button for the door to open and let whoever was coming in to join her.

The doors parted, and it wasn't Amy or one of her nurses.

It was Eve Harrison.

In medical scrubs. Covered in blood splatter.

A lot of it.

"Thanks, Doc," she said, stepping into the elevator, a smile on her face. She looked like a psychopath who'd just finished murdering a houseful of people.

It wouldn't surprise Megan if she had.

She was the last person Megan wanted to talk to.

"Ms. Harrison," Megan said.

"Eve," she said.

Megan glanced at her out of the corner of her eye. "Eve." She pressed the button for the basement level three, where the vampires were.

Eve leaned over and hit the second floor. Blood smeared on the button.

Megan shivered, her doctor side wanting to contain the area and sanitize. But she'd pretty much have to sanitize Eve as well.

"Rough day?" Megan asked.

"Shit happens," Eve replied, and she tipped her head to the side. "Why does nobody look at each other in the elevator?"

"Pardon?" Megan asked.

"No one looks at each other on the elevator. We all just stare at the metal doors, waiting for the box to carry us where we want to go."

Eve ran her hands through her hair.

"Deep thoughts for the end of a shift," Megan said.

"For you. I'm going into job number two, thanks."

"So, this is a job for you? The vampires?" she asked. "No different than any other contract job?"

"Well, not really. Because in the end, I'm probably going to kill them all anyway."

The elevator door opened, and she stepped out.

"Bye," she said, just as happy as a clam.

Megan really couldn't stand her. Her lack of value of life frustrated Megan. Of course, she didn't know too many sheldevak who had any value on mortal life.

After all, the damn creatures ate souls.

Thank goodness she got off on a different floor. Maybe she had other business to attend to.

Which made Megan wonder, what else could Eve Harrison be doing for Jackstone? Or maybe it was something smaller and personal, for James Henrick.

Did she want to know?

Megan shook her head.

The elevator stopped on the proper floor, and she headed down the gray hallway to the apartment the vampires shared.

It wasn't fancy or decorative down here. It was just temporary housing for mythicals who needed a place.

A perfect spot for vampires without a home.

She knew enough about that.

She reached their door and was about to knock, but the door popped open.

"Oh, it's you." Travis Collins said. He looked much better. Clean, shaved, and hair buzzed off. "Hi, Doc."

"You look nice."

He grinned. "Thanks. Come in. We're doing our studies." He paused for a second. "Do you have to be invited in?"

"It's always polite to be invited in, but no, you don't have to invite me in unless you have wards on the residence."

"Wards? What are those?" he asked.

"Magic spells for protection or prevention or restraint."

"Can we do that?" he asked. "I hadn't read about that."

"With enough training, anybody can do anything.

However, some people have more aptitude toward wards and other magical incantations. Vampires, as a general rule, don't have a lot of magical skills. Though there are always exceptions."

"Are you like a walking encyclopedia of mythical stuff?" Joanie asked. She, like the other vampires, held cups of blood —that coppery smell she knew all too well—and all had open books on their laps, with highlighters.

Well, Joanie had a highlighter. And lots of bright yellow lines on the book's pages.

Megan glanced at her. "I'm a doctor. I kind of have to be."

"More like a vet," Jake Reynolds said as he sipped his blood.

And her breath caught.

He stood there, book in his hand. Coffee cup in the other. He should have looked normal. Like any other guy in the world. He should not have looked like a goddamn walking dream in his T-shirt and pajama pants.

But his slightly blond hair, brushed away from his face, and that guy scruff—he'd trimmed his beard down to just that scruff, and holy hell, he looked hot.

"Pardon?" she asked, even though she was blindsided by his hotness, being called a vet didn't sit well with her.

"You have to know about all species, not just human. Like how vets have to know about all kinds of animals," he said, a shrug of his shoulders.

"Well, you all are animals."

"If we want to be," Jake replied.

Malcomb came out of the bathroom—she hadn't realized he wasn't in the room with all the others—and he was cleanly shaven. "Hey, Doc. Do you know a barber that works at night? I gotta get this mop cut, and I'm not shaving it like Collins."

"Once you shave, you don't ever go back," Collins said.

Whatever strange spell that was weaving between Jake and her was broken by her turning to answer Malcomb's question. "No, I don't. I am sure that Eve or Mr. Henrick would have a suggestion."

Malcomb nodded. "Probably. What brings you down here?"

She pulled her tablet out of her bag and a small lab kit.

Time to get to it. No more oogling. "Just a quick exam to make sure everyone's okay. Grab some blood to test."

"Groovy," Thompson added. "I'll go first. I'm not afraid of your little needles."

There was a little bitty part of her that was disappointed that Jake didn't volunteer first.

HALF AN HOUR LATER, she'd taken everyone's blood except Jake's. Joanie had offered the use of her room, since it had a private bathroom, to let the doc do what she needed.

Maybe last is better, she thought as he came in. Because he almost had a swagger to his step. Sort of, anyway.

"Where do you want me?" His voice screamed those sexy vibes.

"On the bed."

What was wrong with her? Was she that hard up that a vampire—a vampire, after all, ugh—smiled at her, and she wanted to take off his clothes and feel every inch of him?

The corner of his mouth rose in a smile. One of those smiles that looked ornery and a little horny.

Gah, could he hear her thoughts?

Was he one of those vampires?

Shit.

Or was it her, broadcasting her thoughts to him? Being

this close to the full moon? It was in just a few days, could she just be reading more into everything?

He started taking off his shirt.

She just stared, because, well, hell. He was beautiful.

He really, really was. Even in her dreams, he didn't look this good. And yep, she had dreams and nightmares about him. No denying it really. It was him. Probably why her wolf kept wanting to roam so much. To get away from the damn nightmares.

They weren't letting up.

Which couldn't be a good sign.

Jake sat down on the bed. Like right in the middle.

She didn't move. Because she knew what she wanted to do. What her wolf wanted her to do, anyway.

And it wasn't attack him, either.

Okay, so it was 'attack' but not the bad kind. The good kind. The really good kind that involved feeling him and all his—

"Doc," he said, his voice low.

She blinked. And probably turned a thousand shades of red, her cheeks so hot. If he could read her mind, he'd so be getting a vision.

Instead, she sat still and patted the bed. "Over here," she said, brushing the edge of the bed, closer to where she was.

He scooted over.

Very close to her.

His leg brushed hers. "Here?"

Their gazes met.

"Here," she said.

"Whatever you want, Doc."

She put her hand on his shoulder. To check him. She swore that was what she was doing. Checking him all out by running her hands all over him. Because she needed to see how firm his pectoral muscles were. And the way his spine felt.

He tipped his head down as she stroked his spine, up to his head.

And sighed.

She met his gaze. "Am I hurting you?"

He met her gaze. "Never."

She stared into his light eyes. There was a moment.

A second.

He leaned in.

She leaned in.

The door flung open. "Dude, I hear Eve coming! Hurry up!"

Jake glanced at the door. Snarled at Collins.

Megan sighed. "I'm sorry. I…" she took his arm. "Let me get the blood sample."

In a few seconds, she had what she needed for the tests.

Jake put on his shirt while she packed up her things.

"Doc, I—"

She raised her hand. "You don't need to say anything." And neither did she as she hurried away. Whether it was the desire or something else, she didn't know. And she didn't want to.

Werewolves didn't date vampires.

10

"We have an assignment," Eve Harrison said. She ran her hand over her hair. "And sorry for the smell. I didn't get to change before I came."

Fresh blood covered Eve.

Overwhelming and robust, the scent of it pulled at Jake's cravings, tugging him like a seductive friend. He clenched his hand tighter around his coffee mug of warmed blood.

Not as deep as the desires he'd felt when he'd been alone with Doc, but that was another thing. A think he'd seriously love to explore, but could he?

After all, the lore all said vampires and werewolves didn't mix. What it meant, he wasn't sure, but he certainly wanted to see.

And he hadn't wanted a female—really wanted one—in at least a decade.

Jake sipped his blood.

Focus on the task...

Drink your blood.

He knew now that bagged blood worked, but faced with both, he would much rather have the fresh blood. But he held still, not letting the cravings overpower his common sense.

He glanced at his friends.

Joanie was smiling like she smelled a warm cookie. They all wore a similar look, the scent of fresh blood did that to them.

But no one moved toward her. Regardless of the craving of the smell, Jake had no reason to attack. He wasn't hungry. Aside from the knee-jerk reaction to the smell, anyway.

Collins broke the ice. "You have blood on you."

She sighed. "I do." She was dressed oddly from how they usually saw her—in, of all things, medical scrubs. Like cute, girly ones. With little bunnies on them. Besides the blood splatters on it, anyway.

That was, at least, very Eve.

But not pink bunnies. She looked normal. Could be walking around any humans, and no one would notice her.

Jake scanned her, expecting to see the outline of some weapon under the baggy clothing, but nothing was there.

Odd.

"Why are you covered in blood?" Thompson asked, his voice almost like he was comforting a child.

And it gave Eve pause. She licked her lips, looked away, then back again. "Because a human died in front of me today. It was messy."

Thompson raised his eyebrow.

"Thought we didn't kill humans," Malcomb said. "Isn't that part of what all this is about? Us being good little vampires, who protect humans rather than kill them?" Malcomb still wasn't crazy about this—he acted like, as he read the books and learned stuff, that he expected to get his own castle somewhere in Transylvania to terrorize the townspeople or something.

"That's what all those damn books say," Collins added.

"Can't go anywhere, can't do anything, can't terrorize some little town in the Pacific Northwest."

"The yeti will fucking destroy you," Eve countered.

"What chapter is that?" Joanie asked, reaching for her highlighter.

"The one marked 'Yeti,'" Eve replied. Though there might have been a bit of a smile on her face when she said it.

"Lovely, more reading," Collins replied.

Jake glanced at Collins.

Collins just wanted to get out of the Jackstone basement.

"Yeah, but who did you kill?" Malcomb asked. "Or is this a case of 'Do what I say, not as I do'?"

She glared at him. "I didn't kill anyone. But a human did die. End of discussion."

Thompson took a step toward Eve. "Are you all right?"

"I'm fucking perfect. Thanks. Now it's time for you to do your goddamn jobs," she snarled and put her hands on her hips. "You have an assignment."

Jake raised his eyebrow.

Thompson stepped back.

And Eve laid out the basics of their first mission.

11

*J*ake picked up his cell phone and held it out in front of him like he was one of those arrogant fuck boys who thought the whole world wanted to know what his phone conversation was about.

Not that the phone was actually on.

It was just a cover. Prevented him from looking crazy when he spoke to the team on coms in the middle of this reasonably crowded bar. One of those little things he picked up along the way. Surveillance and blending in seemed to run in his veins.

What was left of them, anyway.

Inhaling a breath revealed the lusty desire that seemed to permeate the bar's walls. He ran his hand over his freshly shaved chin. He'd had just enough time after Eve left to clean up before coming out.

Getting out of the basement was nice. Seeing the sky— while it wasn't daylight, it was still sky, and that did make everyone feel less like a prisoner.

Probably why he liked hanging out with the werewolf that kept showing up outside every night.

A woman at another table glanced at him, a sultry look on her face.

He gave her the fuck boy nod, then spoke, like he was talking on the phone.

"Check one," he said.

No one in the bar would hear what Jake was saying, but as long as he blended into the crowd, that's what mattered.

He was the man on the floor, dressed in everyday clothing, sitting alone at a table.

The rest of the team was around the room.

"Clear," came Collins's voice in the earpiece.

"Clear," came Joanie's reply as well. They both were in suits, looking very much like bodyguards on the inside of the bar, circling the perimeter. They stuck out because they were supposed to.

"Clear," came Thompson, who was outside.

"So fucking bored," came Malcomb. "Who the hell decided you got to sit inside, and I was stuck out here."

"I did Six, and hopefully you stay bored," Jake replied.

Malcomb grunted.

He hated being called Six. But he was damn good at watching all of their backsides. Hence him being on the roof of the building. Watching.

"Fuck you, Seven," Malcomb countered.

Jake shook his head. Malcomb was a whiny fuck sometimes.

Especially since Jake's rank of an E-7 was one level higher than Malcomb's E-6 from way back in their pre-vampire days.

Even now, though, the military thing was still so ingrained in all of them.

Jake glanced at the stage. "We're just supposed to make sure nothing happens to Miss Larissa." On said stage, Larissa

Warner held a microphone as she smiled and jumped around, getting the crowd near the stage moving.

Though it was a karaoke bar, the small dance floor had a good number of people grinding away, and Larissa, as the emcee for the bar's festivities, kept the energy up.

Overall, people seemed to be having a really great time. There didn't seem to be any crazy exes lurking anywhere.

Was this what their existence would be now? Protecting humans and mythicals from crazy exes? Especially when the exes were mythicals?

Jake hoped this was just a test to see if they'd behave.

Test or no, he and his team, they'd do the job.

No matter what.

So now they waited for someone to cause a problem.

A glass hit the table.

Jake looked up, wondering what woman he'd have to shoo away.

Dr. Criger stood there. "Hi." Not in scrubs or a doctor's coat, or with a stethoscope. Her hair fell down over her shoulders, and her eyes seemed brighter than usual. Very pretty, in fact.

All of her did.

More than pretty.

Hot as hell in her little black dress with it's one white stripe that sort of wrapped around her. He itched to run his hand along that white stripe, up over her hips, the side of her—

She cleared her throat.

He blinked. "Hi." It took him a second to get back in the moment. Then he remembered manners. Once, before, he'd been taught those. "Please, sit."

"What are you doing here?" Jake asked as she got settled.

"Not working." Her gaze ran over him. "What are you doing here in your civilian finery?"

"Working."

She nodded. "So, no fun for you?"

He shook his head.

"Too bad," she replied and leaned toward him, just a bit.

It was a good cleavage shot.

"You look nice in the button-up shirt," she said. "But you should roll up those sleeves a little."

Jake unbuttoned his cuff and started to roll them up. "Better?" he asked.

She nodded. "Now you can see those nice forearms." She put her hand on him, caressing his bare skin.

And that's when he got a whiff.

The good doctor had knocked back a couple and alcohol-fueled her more primitive side. He could smell the lust rolling off her. And it hit him in his own lustful areas.

Hell.

He did not need this tonight.

His earpiece went off.

"Who's that?" Joanie crackled in his ear.

"Doc," he answered back.

"Yep?" Megan replied.

He realized she thought he was talking to her. "What are you doing here, tonight?" he asked, smiling, but not too much. No need to flash the teeth.

"It's my damned night off. I wanted to get away from…" her gaze landed on him.

"All the vampires in your life?"

"Something like that," she said, taking another drink.

A conversation was normal, right? That made him blend in. Yep. "What is your name? Like your real name. Feel like I should call you something besides Doc."

"Megan," she said and smiled at him.

He smiled. "I like that. Megan. Old but classic. Elegant."

She snorted. "I'm not exactly elegant."

"I wouldn't say that. Long dark hair. Strong jaw. Beautiful brown eyes that seem to glow. Soft and creamy skin. Curves—"

"How can you see my curves? I'm sitting down." Her cheeks got that rosy tint to them again. And her pulse started to strum again.

"I could feel you," he said as he leaned a bit closer to her. "Every time you're near." *Today. In the bedroom.*

He wanted to grab her when she'd been caressing him—and there was no way those touches she gave him were anything other than caresses—and throw her down on the bed and take her hard.

Desire boiled in his veins—more intense than he'd ever known. Alive or dead.

Fuck.

He hated holding back. Especially now.

"Today," he said. "When you were examining me."

"Yeah, well, I get my thrills where I can find them," she said, her cheeks turned an even brighter pink. Then she tipped her head to the side a bit, eyebrow raised. "You clean up pretty damn well, yourself."

She reached up and touched his chin. "You look good with a clean jaw. Better without the shirt, though."

He reached for the shirt button. "Should I?"

She raised her eyebrow. There was more play in her face —not the stuffy doctor.

He wondered if this was just how she was outside of work, or if the drink influenced her more relaxed attitude.

"You look good in your dress."

She snorted. "I couldn't wear a smock or scrubs anymore. Every once in a while, a girl's gotta stop hiding and make herself pretty."

Interesting choice of words...

"What are you hiding from?" Jake asked.

"The goddamn nightmares," she said. Embarrassment washed over her face. "Damn. I didn't mean to say that." She pushed her drink away.

He scooted in a bit, so he could hear her. Good enough excuse anyway. And if her slightly accelerated pulse was anything to go by, she noticed his adjustment as well.

Speaking of adjustments, he may need to shift these pants soon.

"What nightmares?" Jake asked, very close to her. He could feel her body heat. It was intense and sexy.

He wanted to play doctor. Check her over too.

"Nightmares. It's a wolf thing," she whispered in his ear, the air warm on his cheek. And he felt it go straight to his pants.

Damn.

Woman.

Wolf.

Fuck.

He turned to look in her eyes. The lids were hooded in desire. She smiled this sultry grin that ran straight—

"What's a damn wolf thing?" Malcomb asked. "Are you fucking picking up mythicals, Jake?"

Goddamn Malcomb!

He gritted his teeth, the fangs had grown long, and he suddenly really wanted to test and see how far he could push the "can't kill the same species" thing.

"Jealous?" Jake countered, tearing his gaze from the good doctor, and back around the bar, looking for, well, he wasn't sure what, but he didn't want to miss something.

"We're working. Did you forget?" Malcomb fired back. The static on Malcomb's com changed, and Jake was pretty sure he was on his way inside.

"Hold your post," Jake whispered.

"Fuck you. This is utter bullshit, Reynolds, and you know it."

"Calm down, Malcomb," Thompson added.

Shit. His team was falling apart.

"Do. Your. Jobs. That's an order," Jake said, through gritted teeth. He glanced at Dr. Megan. She was watching him.

"I should go," she said when he met her gaze.

"You're fine," Jake said. "Stay right here."

She shook her head. "I shouldn't be here, anyway. I need to get home."

"I'll take you," Jake blurted out.

And his ear almost erupted with the commentary from the rest of the team. He regretted the words as soon as he said them. Malcomb was about to have a coronary.

Or explode or something.

"You're sweet," Megan said. She gestured to the stage. "But Amy's here. The nurse?"

Jake nodded, of course, he remembered her.

"She'll give me a ride," Megan continued. She fluffed her hair over her ears, and if he wasn't mistaken, she was putting something *in* her ears as well.

Jake focused on the stage.

Sure enough, Amy was accepting the mic from Larissa, and a slow, soulful ballad started to play.

"Do you sing?" Jake asked Megan, pointing to the stage.

She shook her head. "Not born with that talent. I would clear the place out if I sang." She almost yelled it at him, confirming for him that she must have put something in her ears.

Wow.

Was Amy that bad of a singer?

Joanie's voice crackled in his head. "Reynolds, Malcomb just came in."

Jake sighed and glanced over his shoulder at Malcomb. He should have got up and confronted him. That's what he should have done.

That would have been the correct, leader-like thing to do. Because they had jobs to do.

Nurse Amy's first notes came out, and holy hell, if his focus didn't immediately snap directly to her. A powerful draw. Not desire exactly, but well, attention. He couldn't look away; it was like he'd been hypnotized.

This isn't normal, he thought. But the part of him that realized it was distant from the moment, everything was focusing on Amy as she sang.

Out of the corner of his eye, he saw Megan lean in and put her arm around him.

Whatever. It didn't matter.

All that mattered was Amy and her voice. It filled him with such emotion, so much soul and desire and pain and love and...

He couldn't ignore it. He felt alive. So enrapt in her voice, that he twitched when the woman—Megan—that's who it was—touched his ear.

And then it was over. As suddenly as it began, it ended.

He blinked and looked around.

Everyone in the bar was staring at Amy. Like everyone.

Except for Megan. Instead, the good doctor was watching him, any sense of her being inebriated had vanished.

He glanced at her. "What was that?"

"That's Amy's voice. To those who are susceptible, she will hypnotize them for a bit while she sings."

"Everyone looks susceptible."

She shrugged. "Most are, to a certain degree. Humans, anyway. And some mythicals, but not all."

"And why am I?"

"I suspected it when you all were brought into the hospital, considering your comas. I wondered if it had something to do with the mental charm you'd been put under before, but I wasn't positive."

Jake gritted his teeth. Was that what all this was, this mission? To test and see if he would get hypnotized by a singing, well, whatever the hell Amy was. "What can I do about it?"

She shrugged. "Earplugs. Or headphones would probably work too. Something to block the sound." She tipped her head to the side. "Wear two earpieces instead of one when you all do your jobs. Then you won't be bothered by that kind of thing."

As the song ended, Jake noticed the bar had come back to life. He glanced at Amy, who handed the mic to Larissa and then glanced at Megan.

"Is there even a job tonight? Or did you set this up?" He waved his hand.

She shook her head. "I didn't set anything up."

"She's some kind of siren, I guess, and you just happened to be here with her, when we were?" Jake didn't believe a word of her story. Seemed a bit too contrived for his beliefs.

She glared at him. "I came to the bar for a goddamn drink. Amy was here. I was here. You were here. It's not like this was a set-up."

He raised his eyebrow. "You see why I'm suspicious."

"That's your problem, not mine," she replied and shifted like she was going to get up.

"Hey there, Doc," Malcomb said, leaning across the table. "Welcome to the party. What brings you to the bar, hmm?"

"I could listen to my friend sing. You?" she gestured to Amy, who was approaching the table.

Amy took a seat next to Malcomb. He straightened up, looking much more polite than he did at first.

Malcomb's gaze ran over Amy.

"Hi," she said, her blonde hair sort of waving around her face. She glanced at Malcomb. "How are you feeling?"

He nodded. "Good. You? You look good. Sound good."

She smiled.

"You sing good," Malcomb said.

"Thank you," she replied, smiled at him again, kind of like how someone smiled at a nervous child, then glanced at the doctor. "Are you about ready to go?" she asked.

Megan nodded. "Sure, if you are." Her gaze landed square on Jake again. "I've seen what I wanted to see."

Jake raised his eyebrow. "So it was a set-up,"

"Call it taking advantage of an opportunity."

"I'm not sure I like being taken advantage of," Jake retorted.

She leaned in just a bit. "Are you sure?"

He was about to reply when a man walked up to the table, headed straight for Amy.

"You," he said, putting his hand on her shoulder.

"Hey," she said, pulling away.

"Come on, dance with me," the guy said.

She shook her head. "No, thank you. You go on now."

He got more aggressive.

Pawed at her again.

Malcomb wasn't having that.

"She said no," Malcomb said and shoved the man back.

Hard.

He hit the floor and slid.

And Malcomb leaped.

The fight was on.

Jake just sat there.

"Stop it!" Amy cried out, her eyes wide and wild, glancing at Jake. "Stop him from doing that!"

Jake shook his head.

"Disturbance," Joanie sounded off in his earpiece.

"Fall back. It's Malcomb."

"Uh," Joanie said. "You sure?"

"Yep."

Malcomb got three good punches onto the guy before the real bar bouncers got to them. And what hits they were—the guy was going to be minced meat before long. The bouncers were sure earning their pay tonight.

Though really, he should speak to Isaac privately about his temperament when it came to women.

"Don't you think you should do something?"

Jake shook his head. "Malcomb can deal with his own shit."

Amy was pleading and trying to explain things to the bouncer, while another one hauled Malcomb outside.

"Why aren't you helping him?" Megan asked.

Jake's gaze darted around the bar. "Because of that." He gestured toward the emcee, the woman they were supposed to be protecting.

Larissa was being shoved by a man—a werewolf, from his widow's peak—and tugged away from the stage.

"Target acquired," Jake said, and headed toward the stage.

Sure enough, the werewolf must have been lying in wait for a distraction, to get a moment sort of alone with Miss Larissa. Now that Malcomb had given him that distraction, he attacked the girl.

Jake fought the wake of the crowd facing Malcomb to get to the girl. He was almost to Larissa and her attacker when he got bumped.

He turned.

Joanie and Travis.

He gestured to the sides, and he'd take the middle. They'd get this guy.

And quick.

Jake took a few more steps.

And the attacker looked right at him.

"Hey man," Jake said.

The guy tugged Larissa into his arms. "Get lost, this don't concern you."

Jake shook his head. "Think so, man," Jake said. "Really."

The girl shook, her eyes wide with fear. And yep. There was that smell.

The guy growled.

Like crazy growl. His face morphed.

Larissa cried out.

Jake advanced.

The guy lurched at Jake. Metal shined in his hand. A knife.

"It's gonna be okay," Jake said.

She glared at Jake. "Who the hell are you, anyway?"

The guy thrust the blade into Larissa's side, just enough to make her bleed. "I don't give a fuck who this bastard is. He's got nothing to do with you and me."

She cried out. "Stop it, please. I'll—I'll—" she screamed.

"Shut up. You had your chance. Now it's my turn!" The guy shoved the knife into her side again.

"Put her down. You wanna fight? Fight me," Jake said, moving in.

"Fuck you."

He didn't see the attack coming from the sides.

Joanie got a hold of Larissa, just as Collins slammed the guy in the head.

"Go," Jake said, gesturing to Joanie.

He helped Collins.

Slam.

Slam

Stab.

The guy went stiff.

And vanished in a puff of ash, sort of fluttering in the air.

Jake raised his eyebrow at Collins, who stood there, knife in his hand, still in the position where he'd stabbed the guy.

"Case closed," Collins said.

12

Sweat dripped down Jake's face.

Sparring with Malcomb. Determined to be good.

To be better.

If the ass-chewing they got when they returned to Jackstone had anything to do with it, they had a long way to go.

Evidently, killing another mythical in plain sight of humans was against code.

Go figure. They appreciated them stopping the bad guy but didn't like how it was done.

Felt more and more like the military every day. He did have some concerns regarding how mythicals operated.

The minutiae of it all.

Though all those thoughts swirled away as they practiced punches, kicks, leaps, and general combat training. The physical activity, in a big, open room helped remind Jake that he wasn't just a monster who drank blood. Physical combat was simple enough, regardless of the species.

A punch was still a punch.

With every swing, Reynolds felt his humanity coming back. His soldier coming back. A part of himself he missed.

It felt good to be moving. To be physical. To be practicing but not fighting. No wondering if the next fight would be the last.

"Come on, *Seven*. Move," Malcomb taunted.

Jake grinned.

Punch.

Punch.

Slam

Malcomb was on the mat.

"Watch it, Six."

"Fuck. You did that fast."

"Maybe we have superpowers or something." He held out his hand and helped Malcomb up. Something that he'd wondered about. One of the things he'd been taunted with, before and during the change.

Superpowers.

Strength beyond means. A beautiful gift to a soldier who had a hard time moving after years in combat.

At least his aches had disappeared. That much of Melios's promises had been true. But even though his body didn't hurt to move, the hunger replaced the aches. Always hungry, which made them all always angry and on a hairline trigger. Anything could have set them all off.

And usually did.

Their master had liked it like that.

Now though, not being hungry all the time, things were different. Like having an energy drink, back when energy drinks did something for him.

They wanted to leap tall buildings and all that shit. At least, he did, anyway.

"Yeah, superpowers or something," Jake said, smiling.

They started again.

This time, Malcomb was faster.

Jake hit hard, Malcomb a blur around him as he moved.

"Now that shit's pretty cool," Malcomb said after he rose up. He kept looking at his hands. "I expect them to be on fire. Or pulsing with some weird magic."

Jake nodded because he knew exactly what his friend meant. "Feel almost new," Jake said. A scar on his arm was proof that they weren't all the way new, but mostly new.

Certainly, an improvement.

"You know, there's something weird I noticed last night," Malcomb said.

"What?" Jake asked.

"No guns."

Jake nodded. "I noticed that too."

"I mean, like, no one has them. It's like they don't exist or something."

Jake nodded because he'd seen the same thing. No one seemed to have anything other than a taser. Well, except Eve on her first arrival, she'd had a couple of handguns, but nothing major.

Jake half-expected a place like this to have a whole warehouse arsenal somewhere, like in a movie.

One more disappointment of reality.

"What's that all about?" Malcomb asked. "Doesn't that seem weird?"

"I suppose we could ask," Jake said.

"Ask what?" Eve Harrison said.

Jake glanced at her. "You need a bell or something."

"Now, that would distract from my stealth."

"Exactly."

"What's up, boys?" she asked, arms over her chest. A gleam of sweat was on her brow, and she'd been working hard in the corner with Joanie, teaching her some special moves.

Whatever that walking-on-the-walls thing was they were doing.

"Where are the guns, Eve?" Jake asked.

She blinked.

Smiled.

"Wondered how long it would take you to notice."

"What's the deal?"

"What did Melios tell you about guns?"

"That they were stupid, and only for cowards."

She snorted. "Figures. He didn't respect humans at all."

"What does that have to do with anything?" Malcomb asked. "Are guns not allowed or something?"

"Oh, you can use them. It's just frowned upon. Especially by old ones. Considered a cheap, cowardly way to win a fight."

Jake glanced at Malcomb. "But we can? Because I gotta say, I'd be a lot more comfortable with a pistol on my hip than not."

She shook her head. "No. Swords, blades, knives. Combat weapons. No guns."

"Why?" Malcomb asked.

"Ballistics," she said. "You shoot a vampire when he disappears, the bullet still is there. Crime scene investigators don't like to find bullets in piles of ash. It looks suspicious."

"Wait," Jake said.

"Do you mean we can kill fellow vampires with guns?" Malcomb took the words out of his mouth.

"No guns," Eve said. "I mean it."

"Sure, whatever you say," Jake replied.

She nodded and walked away, and Jake and Malcomb glanced at each other.

"Interesting development."

Malcomb nodded. "Raises questions."

"Yes, it does. About how things really work. And what's really expected of us."

"If this is where we should be," he said quietly, glancing around the gym. Jake noticed that the others were working out hard, not paying a lot of attention to them.

Maybe they didn't hear the conversation.

"Beats the alternative."

Malcomb shook his head. "But did we trade one war for another?"

"What choice do we have? We were on the wrong side of the last one. Maybe being on the right side will end better."

"How do we know, though. How do we know this is any better than being under Melios? Maybe we'll have to do some fucked up shit here, too."

Reynolds had the same worries. After what all they went through before—coercion to join, then complete devotion to Melios's commands. And in Melios's world, if it didn't excite him, it would die.

Melios did have one thing in common with this new boss, Eve. Justice was quick, and there was no room for negotiation.

"Okay, bloodsuckers," Eve said. "Time to eat."

Jake shook his head. "I'm fine." About that time, his stomach rumbled.

"Sure about that?" She smirked and crossed the room. Dr. Criger—back in her doctor's smock—had come in with a cart of bagged blood.

She pushed the little cart across the gym floor, and the tires squealed on the shiny floor.

Jake grinned. He wanted more time with her. More moments without doctor's coats and buttoned up sleeves.

"Hi," he said as he walked over, and gave her a smile.

She paused; her eyes wide for a second.

Shit. Did that show his teeth? Would it make him look like he wanted to take a bite out of her?

Fuck.

No smiling.

"How are you? I'm glad you got home okay."

"Yes, I did, thank you." She glanced down for a second before meeting his gaze again. "How are you?"

"Better and better," he said. "How do I look?" He raised an eyebrow, modeled one of those flexing-bodybuilder poses, and gave her, he hoped, his most winning, sexy smile. One without teeth, anyway.

She smiled back at him. Her eyes twinkled. "In the light of a gym? Not bad."

"Better than in the dark?"

Her head tipped to the side, and she had this sultry look on her face for a moment. "Everyone looks better in the dark."

"Then maybe we need to spend some time in the dark."

"We already did." She glanced away from him. Looked down. He couldn't help noticing the way the tint of her cheeks changed, ever so slightly. And he heard her pulse quicken a tiny bit.

He didn't dare say any of the cheesy pickup lines roaming around in his head. Though if they made her laugh…

He brushed off the thought.

Looked down. He felt awkward and bumbling, like he'd never talked to a woman before, which was such bullshit. Yet here he was, acting like he was still in school or something.

When in doubt.

K. I. S. S.

Keep it simple, stupid.

The only worthy piece of advice he'd ever got from his wayward father.

He gestured to the cart. "Got something for me?"

"Yes. I heard you all were down here. Thought you might be a bit peckish and would like something to drink. Help keep you in good health. After your first assignment and all," she smiled at everyone as the rest of the team crowded around the little cart. Each person got an oversized pouch that resembled an IV bag, but with straws in the bottom.

"Like a juice bag," Collins said. "I feel like I'm back in grade school." He bumped Joanie's elbow. "So, can we go to recess now? Can we?"

"Not until you finish your math."

"Aww!"

Joanie smirked. "You're such a dork."

"You wouldn't want me any other way."

They walked away, drinking.

Thompson and Malcomb stayed by the cart with Jake and Megan, drinking their blood.

"Ahh, this is good," Thompson said. "Refreshing." He nodded at her. "Thank you."

"You're welcome," she said, smiling at Thompson.

Again, Jake felt that pang of irritation at Thompson for getting her attention.

Though he didn't seem to have it for long.

She shifted from one foot to the other and gestured to Collins and Joanie, her voice low. "So, if I may ask, are they mated?"

"Why wouldn't you be able to ask?" Jake asked, matching her cadence. And he leaned a bit closer to her as he spoke.

She glanced at him. "I didn't know if your, uh, nest, had privacy rules. Or if there were special arrangements." She turned more toward him. And that quickening pulse he'd heard before, it got even more noticeable.

Like she was nervous.

He raised his eyebrow. "Special arrangements?"

Her cheeks flushed. Like before, but pinker. Different.

"She is the only woman in your group. Some mythicals have, well, other arrangements with females in their groups."

Jake blinked.

And realized she meant sexual relationships. Sharing partners, and all of that. Their former master had no qualms about sharing his partners. However, none of them, including Jake, mirrored their sire's attitude on that score.

Jake preferred his own conquest.

He didn't share well. None of them did.

His gaze darted to Joanie, and he shook his head. "No. No, we do not have arrangements with Joanie." Like Joanie would allow such a thing, anyway. She'd kick any of their asses for even suggesting it.

"Some vampires make those kinds of nests."

"I know," Jake said. He knew all too well how vampires sexualized eating. Melios had always claimed it charged the blood, made it stronger somehow.

Jake didn't think it made it that much better.

Of course, Melios had also said bagged blood wouldn't sustain them.

"What are you two whispering about?" Malcomb asked, staring at them.

"Why you smell like old shoes all the time. If it's something that can be cured," Jake popped off.

"Hardy har har," Malcomb said. "So we're clever now? We're all smart and charming and clever?" He waved his hand in the air between him and Thompson. "Because I don't remember getting that memo. Did you get that memo?"

"Nope," Thompson said, grinning. His teeth didn't peek out too much. Maybe Jake could smile without looking like he was going to take a bite of someone. Might have to practice in the mirror.

And yes. Vampires could see themselves just fine in mirrors.

One of the big things every one of them did after they got settled was some much-needed grooming. He was quite happy shave off his scruff.

A barber was next on the list. Jake wasn't a fan of his hair all the way to his shoulders.

He glanced at the doctor. "You asked a question."

"Yes. About those two." The blushing in her cheeks was dissipating, and surprisingly, Jake was sorry to see it go. She looked pretty with some rose in her cheeks.

The couple in question was practicing leaping. Joanie was trying a running approach—running up the wall, and doing a side flip, landing on her feet.

"Whoa!" Jake clapped for Joanie.

Thompson whistled, and Malcomb clapped as well.

"Great job, Joanie!" Malcomb yelled.

Collins was losing his mind. Grabbed her and yanked her into a bear hug. Then they started doing a series of high-fives.

"Are they?" she asked.

"Them? Mated? No. Brother and sister. Basically," Thompson said. "They were in S.W.A.T. together. Before," he said, and sipped on his blood.

"Did all of you know each other when you were mortal?" Megan's gaze darted to Jake.

Jake shook his head. "Not personally, no."

"You knew me," Malcomb said.

Jake shrugged. "I try not to tell people that," he glanced at Megan. "Gives them a false impression of me."

"What impression is that?"

"Yeah, what the fuck does that mean?" Malcomb asked.

"It means, you're a big asshole, and he doesn't want people thinking he's an asshole too," Thompson said.

"Fuck you."

"Gentlemen please. Language," Jake said.

Malcomb hit Reynolds's arm. "What the actual fuck, dude?"

"We are in the presence of a lady. You should mind your manners."

"Who are you trying to impress?" Malcomb said.

Thompson hit him in the arm. "Come spar with me."

"I'm not done with this butthole."

Thompson grabbed him. "Come. On." He practically dragged Malcomb away.

"What's that all about?" Megan asked.

Jake shook his head, amused at his friend. "I think he was trying to let us talk alone."

"Oh." She glanced at him. "Did you want to talk to me alone? Are you feeling okay?"

"I feel fine," he said.

"What was it then?"

Jake went for broke. "Go out with me."

"What?"

"Like on a date."

She raised her eyebrow. "You buying?"

"Probably." If everything was still as it should be, then yeah, he'd buy. If not, well, that he'd deal with.

"Okay, mister. We can do, uh..." she hesitated briefly, "how about coffee?"

"That sounds safe." And cheap. Worked for him.

"Well, do I really want to entice a vampire?"

"Can a werewolf hold her own?"

"Oh yeah."

.

13

*T*he coffee shop wasn't anything particularly fancy, and on a weeknight, it wasn't horribly packed.

Megan wasn't sure why she was even there, to be honest. A date with a patient, especially a vampire patient, was bizarre.

For her to do it? Even crazier.

Yet here she was. Letting Jake hold the door open, pull out her chair, and buy her coffee. It was so old fashioned.

And damn her girly parts for being so taken by all of it. She'd gotten home last night, hoping the attraction she'd felt around the vampire was just from drinking and loneliness, and too much time thinking about him.

And then there he was, in her space, looking all hot in his civilian clothing.

With rolled-up cuffs.

Which he wore again tonight, revealing some strong wrists. Tonight, she was sober enough to appreciate it. But also, that same soberness brought forth other questions.

Like when the heck did wrists become attractive? And what in the actual hell was wrong with her? She shouldn't be so interested in anyone, especially a patient, but she couldn't help it. Every time she was around him, it got stronger.

Surely, he wasn't trying to mind-whammy her, was he? Had that nest he'd been in before taught him some psychic tricks?

She looked into his light eyes and thought *Damn.*

If he was manipulating her, she sure couldn't tell.

Instead, they had fun. Talked about benign things, like where she went to school—what she could say about it, anyway, she did. While no mythical law (spoken or unspoken) said they couldn't discuss elements of magic and mythical life in the presence of humans, it was highly frowned upon if they did. Keeping the humans ignorant of the monsters walking among them, and all of that.

Jake seemed to respect that and managed to dance around the subject enough. He talked about his military career. About family. About boring things that anyone would talk about on a date.

It should have been the most lackluster date in the world.

It wasn't though. It was light and fun. It was even sensual when he'd look at her a certain way. Shivers ran through her, all the way to her toes.

And back up to other parts.

She couldn't stop staring at him. The way his jawbone was shaped, how his eyes sat so deep in his face—sensual, not crack-head deep. He looked like a carving. A piece of art from a historical realm.

His pale skin accentuated the features, and the light of the coffee shop seemed to make it even more prominent. A couple of women at another table commented on it. Megan sort of let her gaze flick back to them, not appreciating their evaluation of her date, but she didn't want to start anything in the middle of a coffee shop.

He's mine, ladies.

Hands off.

The beast under her skin growled.

Part of her wanted to step back, and question where this was coming from, but analysis meant results, and she wasn't sure she was ready to know what this was between her and a vampire.

She focused on him. On his situation. Not on her feelings.

"Are you getting used to the apartment?" she asked.

Again, with the lackluster conversation.

Still, she couldn't help it. She wanted to know all the things about Jake.

"We are comfortable for now," Jake replied, sipping on his coffee. He winced as he did. "Gah," he muttered. "I used to live on this."

"It'll come in time," Megan said. "It takes getting used to, so I've been told. But you'll adapt. Everyone does."

"I'm trying," he said.

"Don't push it. You'll get there."

He nodded. "Feel like a fawn trying to walk, now that this is gone." He waved his hand around his head, and she took that to mean the pressure or the voice in his head that had been his sire.

Whatever the hell that had been.

"I still have no idea what he did to you, exactly."

"We may never know."

She shook her head. "We may not."

He glanced at his watch.

"You got another appointment?" she asked.

He shook his head. "Eve usually shows up about midnight or so. I wanted to be back before she comes by with our latest homework."

"Sure, that makes sense. This is practically your morning."

He smiled. "Yeah. The sun goes down, and I come alive."

"Do you?"

"Want to find out?" He gave her that look again, and it went straight through her. In all the right ways.

She smiled. "Maybe."

She leaned in a bit.

"Are you tempting me?"

She licked her lips. "What would you do if I was?"

"I always do what my doctor says."

"Promises, promises." She tried to pretend this little conversation wasn't affecting her, but wow, it was.

Time to shift gears. "But first, I gotta know though, where did you get the money? Did you go rob a bank?" She kind of hoped not, but wasn't sure she'd be against the idea, considering the old school chivalry vibes he was giving off. He held her chair and everything—and that was an adventure sitting down, she'd not actually had a guy do that before.

There's an art to sitting, and someone helping you with your seat. Who knew?

"Not exactly."

She raised her eyebrow. "Do you have some secret asset?"

"I kept the change," he said.

"Pardon?"

He smiled, but carefully, not showing his teeth. "When I would be tasked with a job, I would usually be given cash for any expenses incurred. I kept the change."

"Resourceful."

He shrugged. "There were enemies around. I was just reading the terrain."

"And now?"

He shrugged. "Still collating data."

"Are you going to stay?"

"If there's a good reason to stay," he said.

"You can always find reasons if you look for them."

Something she knew from experience. There were answers to anything if one looked for them.

He nodded. "I don't know where I'd go. I shouldn't be here anyway, from what I've been told."

"Do you know why?"

"We surrendered at the last second, I think. It might have been the moment he died. I just know that in my head, everything changed. Like perception changed."

"Probably his mind control releasing."

He nodded. "Probably. I just knew where I was, and why I was there, but the reasons suddenly didn't matter. Not like they had before."

She shifted and stroked the edge of her coffee cup. Jake's eyes remained on her cup. And the way he looked at her fingers, desire seemed to radiate off him.

"What is this?" he asked, glancing at her.

"What?" Though she knew exactly what he was asking.

"This, between us."

"There's nothing between us."

She wanted to kick herself, for as soon as the words left her mouth, she saw Jake deflate.

"There can't be anything between us," she said.

"What's the difference?" Jake asked. "Because I don't want to waste your time or mine."

"One is a lack of something. The other is an admission, but a barrier."

"So which is it? A lack, or a barrier."

"A barrier."

14

*B*arriers can be broken.

That's what Jake told himself when he walked Megan out to her car.

It's what ran through his head when he reached for her car door to open it for her. When she told him they couldn't do things because he was her patient. Or when she used the excuse of being a werewolf, and he was a vampire.

They can be broken...

Which made Jake spend a few hours digging through their little reference book about vampires and werewolves mating. Eve showed up at one point, told everyone to do laps and practice running on the walls for a while, then she disappeared.

He had plenty of time to research.

Now, in the pre-dawn hours, Jake sat outside on the little perch he'd been sitting on every night just before dawn, thinking.

He opened the piece of paper he'd written out with all the reasons he'd found showing they could be together. And he'd found a lot of them.

Between his notes from their Balance Mandate books—none of which said vampires and werewolves couldn't be together—and going through thousands of websites, looking for myth and historical records hinting to the possibility a werewolf and a vampire could be together, he had quite an argument.

Because it didn't matter how much he told himself to not think about her like that, all he wanted was Megan.

He was drawn to her, unlike he'd ever experienced with anyone. Was that part of being a vampire? Feeling things so strongly? Had this part of himself been repressed before, somehow?

Because nothing felt as intense as the thoughts of her.

It would explain the intensity of the other attachments he'd established—like with the team. With the kid.

The kid.

Hell, just thinking about the child Melios had running around brought a ton of emotions to the surface. He'd practically watched her grow up. It brought a tear to his eye, knowing she was gone.

It saddened him.

She was a kid. She had a chance at life. More than just being a vampire slave or, well, whatever the hell she was for Melios.

Part of his grand plan to take over the world or some shit.

A sound—one he was getting used to hearing—echoed in the quiet.

Flump.

The werewolf was back.

"Hey there, Fluffy," Jake said, immediately petting the wolf's head in that spot behind the ears the wolf loved. "Do you like that? You like Fluffy?" He nuzzled the animal-like he did every night since they met.

He loved the way it smelled. He wasn't sure if the wolf was a boy or a girl, but who cared, really.

"Come on," he said, "let's run."

They didn't go far.

The two of them leaped over the twelve-foot fence with ease, into the large, open, and very private courtyard. It was a training area, or gym or something. Maybe for the humans to have lunch in during the day.

Jake didn't care.

He and Fluffy ran it like pros. He ran, leaping over obstacles, practicing flips and twists. The wolf stayed right with him the whole time, matching him move for move. They were having a blast. Jake even tried some of those wall-walking flip things Joanie had been doing. He didn't yet have quite the ability she had to use the wall like another floor, and he hit the ground hard, slamming on his shoulder.

"Damn," he muttered.

Fluffy ran to his side, nuzzling him. Jake rubbed the animal's head. "It's fine. I'm okay."

The wolf pawed at him a bit.

He hugged on the animal, the two of them wrestling around on the ground. He looked into the eyes of the wolf and saw the intelligence behind them.

"I know they say you don't remember, but I bet you do. At least a little."

The dog growled an affirmative, or so Jake thought.

"Did I tell you I used to have a dog? For a bit, anyway. In the service, I had a military dog. Carrot."

Fluffy huffed disapproval.

"I agree, it was a terrible name. Anyway, Carrot smelled out the bad guys. And the bombs." He looked down, his memories coming back from those days. From that day in particular.

Sights. Sounds. Smells.

"He found one. It had been rigged to run as silently as possible." Jake held up his shirt to reveal the seven-inch scar on his side. "I got out with this. Carrot didn't."

Fluffy's head went down.

"Me too." He stroked the wolf's back. He knew Fluffy wasn't a dog. Or a wolf, really. Yet, it felt like a companion. A trusted friend.

Something Jake needed more of.

"I had my date."

Fluffy's ear perked up.

"I think it went well. Mostly. But she's, I don't know." He looked up at the stars. "Afraid. But I don't think it's of me. It's more of the idea."

Fluffy nuzzled him.

"Doctor Megan needs to want me back," he said. "And not be afraid." He pulled out a piece of paper, with all his notes on it. "I have all these cases. Evidence to show something could work. But I don't know if she'll read them."

The wolf huffed again.

"That's the problem, I think. I am not sure what her barrier is. If it's the species thing, or if it's the immortality thing." He glanced at Fluffy. "Personally, a decade like this, I don't know that I'd want to live forever."

He looked up at the stars again.

"Forever seems like a lot of wasted time."

Fluffy leaped up.

"What?" Jake did too and looked around.

Fluffy growled and started to run off.

He followed, and the wolf leaped out of the courtyard and headed back to where they usually would go in for their snack.

Jake smirked, realizing where Fluffy was going. "You're hungry, huh? Well, I could use a drink myself."

Fluffy led the charge into the building, pausing only where doors needed to be opened.

Jake laughed when the wolf got to his apartment and started pawing at the door. He popped the door open, letting his friend walk on in like the animal owned the place.

As he expected, Joanie, Thompson, and Malcomb were streaming some series they'd found, wrapped up in their show.

Since dawn was coming, it was getting closer and closer to their bedtime, anyway.

"Hey Jake," Joanie said. "Fluffy."

The wolf huffed a response.

Malcomb looked over. "Uh, what the hell is that?"

"Fluffy," Jake replied.

"It's Jake's secret pet he's been feeding the last few nights," Joanie said. "Isn't it cute, it's like he's 12."

"What the absolute fuck. Hitting on women, and now you have a pet wolf?" Malcomb snapped. "Do you need to be relieved of duty?"

"Fuck you," Jake snapped.

Fluffy agreed and growled.

Jake opened the fridge and pulled out some meat from the refrigerator.

"I wondered why we had that," Thompson said. "We can't eat it."

Jake shrugged. "Fluffy likes it." He held it out, and the wolf turned up its nose.

Thompson laughed.

"Really? Just when I was bragging you up, you turn away?"

Fluffy started sniffing around, searching for something.

"Fluffy?"

The wolf nosed open Jake's room and headed inside.

Joanie laughed. "I told you not to feed it."

Jake shrugged. "It's not like it's going to be a wolf forever."

"No, it's probably one of those damn Cold Team members, and they're going to kill you when they wake."

The thought had crossed Jake's mind too.

"I hope you didn't tell it anything important."

Depends on who you ask, Jake thought.

He went into his room, just in time to see the wolf spin twice on his bed and curl into a ball.

He sighed.

"What am I going to do with you? You're in my bed."

The wolf wasn't moving.

He shook his head. "Not like I haven't slept with a dog before." He sighed and gathered up his stuff to go grab a quick shower.

After the cleaning, he crossed the living room back to his bedroom, and Joanie glanced at him. "So, still a wolf in there?"

Jake looked inside. "Yep." Fluffy was still in the same position on the bed. But somehow had managed to take up more space on the bed than before.

He grabbed an extra blanket and pillow and decided he'd just sleep on the floor. He'd slept on plenty. One more wouldn't kill him. Having a bed was nice, but the firmness of the floor was almost comforting.

He'd just laid down when he felt something warm against him.

He opened his eyes.

Fluffy had come onto the floor to join him.

"You crazy animal," Jake muttered. "I kind of hope you're a girl because if you're a boy, this is going to be so awkward later."

He closed his eyes to sleep.

DREAMS HIT HIM.

Hard.

Fast.

Chaos trying to become noise.

Noise trying to become sound.

Sound trying to be heard.

Jake ran.

Hard.

Run fast.

Want.

Need.

Desire.

Long silky legs.

Such soft hair.

Warm. Secure. Safe.

Jake Prey.

Jake Prey

"Jake Prey!"

He jerked, untangling himself from the body that had wrapped around him in sleep.

Because he got his wish. Fluffy was, indeed, a girl.

The naked woman in front of him panted as she jerked the blanket over her body. She brushed her hair from her face.

"Doc?" He asked. "Megan?"

She twitched, her hands immediately pulling at the covers. "What? Where?"

"Shh, it's me. Jake."

Her eyes were wild, and she kept pulling away. "Where am I?"

"Doc, it's me."

Her eyes seemed to focus, and she stopped trembling so hard. "Jake?"

"Yeah."

"What am I doing here?" she asked. She waved her hand. "This is, uh, Jackstone isn't it?"

He nodded again. "The barracks. Apartment." Damn, she was beautiful. Like incredibly stunning to look at.

But he shouldn't be staring at her. It was rude. He reached for his little dresser and pulled out a T-shirt for her.

She slipped the shirt on and wrapped the blanket around her lower half. Still, she trembled as she did.

"How did I get here? Did I… The beast come here?"

He nodded as he scooted toward her and held out his hand. She took it and slid towards him.

"It's okay, I promise. You can trust me," Jake said, and held his arm out to, well, hold her. Hug her. Embrace. Whatever she needed. If she needed anything.

He wasn't sure. New territory and all that.

"I know that," she replied, scooting into him. "But how did the beast know?"

"I have a trusting face," Jake said, internally doing a high five to himself because she did accept his gesture.

She smiled. "You do. But still, I don't really get this. Why would I come here?" she looked around. "And why would you bring me into your home?"

"You have been for a while. Fluffy comes—"

"You nicknamed me Fluffy?"

"You're pretty fluffy."

She looked almost mortified. "I am a badass werewolf that'll rip your head off."

He slid one hand under her hair. "You also really like being pet right here." He caressed the base of her neck up to her head and back down again.

Even in human form she liked it, her head rocked into the touch, and she released a soft sigh.

"You found a weakness."

He leaned in. "I'm good at that."

She met his gaze, and her eyes got that look in them, the one she'd had before that made his pants get tight.

Their lips were close. He could feel her breath.

He wanted to taste her, so much. The desire was so strong.

"Meg—"

She cut him off, leaning in as her lips touched his. It was soft. Then it wasn't. It was hard, and full of need and want, and it became so much more intense.

When did kissing feel like this?

Everything lit on fire. Intense, in a way he'd never known. It was amazing. Incredible.

Alive.

He felt *alive*.

He couldn't remember the last time he felt this kind of energy and desire pulsing through him. He deepened the kiss, wanting to taste all parts of her.

She moaned as she ran her hands through his hair.

He stroked her as they kissed, and she leaned into him.

As she did, she pushed him down to his back. Their lips not separating, at least not at first. He'd do whatever she wanted. If she wanted him on his back, that's what he'd do.

Anything for her.

He kissed her neck, then her throat, tugging at the T-shirt. Her skin was so soft and tasted so good. He wanted to savor every bit of her, to know her in every way he could. His teeth elongated, and he opened his mouth—

She pushed him back. "Not yet," she said, a teasing smile on her face. She pulled the shirt off, almost too slowly, like she was stripping for him. The slow rising of the fabric revealed her breasts, and damn if they weren't perfect in every way. Hell, there wasn't part of her that wasn't perfect.

Every man's dream woman, right there, straddling his cock.

In all her naked glory, with the blanket tossed aside—an afterthought—Megan loomed over him, her body pressing against his in all the right ways. The only thing separating them was his boxer shorts, but much more of the rocking and they wouldn't matter anyway, he'd rip through them.

Her center rubbed right on his cock and holy fuck did it feel amazing. He'd had a fair share of women, and a fair share of women since becoming a vampire, but no one created this kind of response in him.

He rocked his hips into hers, his hand caressing her sides, down and around, feeling her ass. He had to have her.

"I want you."

She rocked harder into him; her eyes almost seemed to glow for a second. "How bad," she whispered.

"So bad."

"Prove it," she said.

He moved his head down, going for those incredible tits. He had to taste those nipples, feel them pebble in his mouth. She moaned, holding his head to her breasts as she rocked against him.

She groaned as he teased her boobs and stroked her ass. He brought his hands around, feeling along the front to her slick folds, and slid a hand between them.

She arched just a little, allowing him to hit her clit, and he did all the things, everything he could stimulate all at once because he wanted her to lose it. To come all over him.

He needed it.

He needed her.

Fuck, he needed her.

She arched back, her hips undulating in his hand, and she came, growling as she did. Her eyes were lighter, brighter as she came.

She'd barely stopped when Jake rolled her over and climbed on top.

"Oh hell," she whispered. Their gazes locked. "Do me hard. Now."

"Yes, ma'am."

He shucked his boxers and scooped her up.

He tossed her on the bed, her hips hanging off the edge. Their gazes met, and she parted her legs.

He grabbed them and pushed them wide before plunging in. Nothing slow, lingering or gentle here.

This was…

Oh fuck.

Hell.

Damn. Shit.

Fuck.

Nirvana…

Fucking nirvana.

He slammed hard into her slick folds. She cried out, and sort of sat up. He dropped her legs and leaned into her.

"God," she moaned.

"Fuck," he replied.

"Yes!" she cried out, as another wave overtook her.

He kept driving into her.

His teeth elongated, and he could feel, see, smell, everything. Her pulse was exploding in her neck, and he was desperate to taste it.

He pushed himself back because he didn't want to—

She grabbed the back of his head. "Do it," she said and bared her neck.

He didn't wait.

He bit her throat.

Blood—her blood—filled him as he orgasmed.

It was truly the most incredible thing in the world.

Like ever.

It would have been the absolute most perfect moment ever if his bedroom door hadn't opened.

"Reynolds, you okay?" Malcomb stuck his head in.

He took one look at Jake and Megan on the bed.

"Shit! Oh! Fuck."

Megan glanced at him, then at Jake. "You need a lock."

"Think so," Jake replied.

AFTER AN HOUR or two of napping/cuddling, Jake woke from another nightmare.

Rather, he woke from another nightmare that Megan was having. Why he knew it was hers, he had no idea, but it was.

Because he'd never had a fear of death. One couldn't be in the military, and do as many of the missions he'd done, and be afraid of dying.

Yet, the dreams tonight were all nightmares about his death.

It had to have something to do with her.

Her eyes fluttered open, and she glanced at him. "Sorry. I seem to always be waking you up."

Jake pressed his hips into hers. "I'm not complaining."

"Again?"

"As much as you like."

She smiled. But she seemed distant. He pulled back.

"Want to talk about it?"

"It just, I don't know how to process everything."

"Process what? That you're my Fluffy?"

She chuckled. "That's there, but low on my list."

He stroked her cheek. "You don't remember anything when you're in wolf form?"

She shook her head. "Not really, no. Most werewolves

don't. Not beyond a few simple memories." She shook her head. "So how long has this been going on?"

"Since I woke up."

"Like every night?" she asked.

"Yep. We're pals."

"You talk to a wolf that you don't even know? Doesn't that seem strange?"

He shook his head. "I talked to my military dog every day. Fluffy is just bigger."

She sighed. "This is the craziest thing. Almost as crazy as the dreams I keep having."

He glanced at her. "Yeah, those crazy dreams. Chaotic and intense."

"How do you know about my dreams?" She narrowed her gaze. "Can you see them or something?"

"Something," he said. "Mega hellish ones. Like scary dangerous. And I don't scare easily."

She stared at him for a minute. Like she was trying to figure something out.

He stroked her shoulder, ran his finger along her collar bone. She stared off in the distance, her mind working something out.

He stroked her throat.

She started to laugh.

He jerked back. "Sorry, didn't mean to tickle you."

"No," she said and laughed again, cackling with that full, belly laugh that shook her shoulders.

He couldn't help grinning. That joyous sound was infectious. Tears even came from her eyes, she laughed so hard.

"Oh, hell," she finally said, wiping tears from her eyes.

"What is so funny?"

"You. Me. All of it."

"I didn't think I was bad," he said.

She smacked him. "Not that." She made herself take a few breaths. "Werewolves have this thing. We have nightmares about our mated one, from the time we meet them."

"Nightmares?" What kind of a fucking curse is that? What sadistic bastard decided that's how werewolves knew their mate?

"It's the way we know. We mate for life, so finding a partner is very serious. The nightmares plague us from the time we meet them until a relationship is bound, or we have sex. And we'll never leave them, not in all our days."

"You've been having nightmares about me," he said.

She nodded. "Ever since you woke up. Every night."

"So, what are you laughing about? Does this mean we're mates?"

She shook her head. "I thought we were, at first."

"I don't understand."

"But because I've spent time with you every night as well, in wolf form, it's my brain, processing the encounters, in the only way it knows. You're always hungry in the dreams. Starving, and you're being hurt."

"Like my life before, I guess."

"Did you talk to me, to the wolf, about it?"

"Sure. Sorting my thoughts and stuff. Seemed safe enough."

She ran her hand over her face. "Jake, I'm not attracted to you. My wolf has been trying to tell me your story."

15

There was nothing quite like walking out from a one-night stand's apartment.

It is literally a thousand times worse, though, when that walk is from a patient's bedroom, in front of his friends, and wearing his clothes.

At least she was already at her place of employment. She could run upstairs and change.

If there was time.

A glance at the clock on the wall told her she was almost an hour late to her shift at the hospital. She didn't run, but she sure walked as fast as she could.

Barefoot.

Up to the hospital.

The calls for her hit like a wall

"Dr. Criger!"

"Dr. Criger! We've been trying to reach you."

And on they went. Nurses, fellow doctors, even patients, were badgering her for consultation. She'd barely got inside her office when Amy came barging in.

"Are you okay?" she asked, and then tipped her head to

the side, her gaze narrowing. "Wait a second. I know that look."

"What look? There is no look." Megan fiddled with her hair, trying to bundle it into her usual top knot.

"You got laid."

"No, I did not," she said, turning away, her cheeks warm as she pulled a fresh set of clothing out of her tiny little closet. Boy, was she glad she'd decided to keep a couple of outfits up at the hospital, just in case she needed a change.

"Bull. I can see it in your gait. Hell, you have a glow."

"It's just pre-full-moon-glow. All werewolves get it." She changed her clothing behind the closet door.

Amy shook her head. "No, they don't. Not *that* glow. Besides, what the hell are you wearing? Men's clothing?"

Megan sighed. "I am obviously running behind. I have patients to see. I don't want to entertain this."

"What the hell, Megan. Entertain this? Since when did I get formal doctor speak? You're talking to me, you know."

She looked at her friend. One of the few friends she really had a. "Look, I did something stupid last night. Really stupid. And I'm not ready to deal with it just yet."

Amy nodded. "Look, I'm here for you when you are." She turned and pulled open the door.

Then the one thing she didn't want to deal with was standing right behind it.

Jake Reynolds.

"We need to talk," Jake said.

Amy's eyes got wide, and she glanced between Jake and Megan.

"This is not the time," she said to Jake.

Amy slipped out of the office, her eyes wide. And she might have given Megan a thumbs-up behind Jake's back.

"I'm not buying it," he said, as the door shut.

"Not buying what?"

"You cannot tell me with what we shared, that there's no attraction between us."

"There's no attraction between us," Megan replied. But she didn't sound very convincing.

Jake didn't seem to be buying it either. "Bullshit."

She raised her eyebrow. "Listen, I have to go see to my patients. Later. We can talk later." She took a step toward him. "What we shared was great. Probably the best I've had in a while."

He might have hissed when she said the last part.

"But I'm not going to fill you full of promises that aren't going to happen. You're a vampire. I'm a werewolf. It just isn't done, Jake."

"Why not?"

"It just isn't."

She walked past him and out into the hospital.

And she was pretty sure he wasn't buying her bullshit, either.

Because she didn't have a reason. Not a good one anyway, besides old, stupid biases.

16

*J*ake really didn't want to see Megan.

So, of course, she walked into the gym that night, looking as beautiful as ever. And damn, did he want to take her back to his room and this time, since no one was there, make her scream his name.

She smiled like nothing had happened as she approached him.

He picked up his towel and patted off his face.

"Doctor," he said.

"Are you available to chat now," she asked, sort of gesturing with her head for him to walk with her.

"Since you didn't greet me with a kiss, I'm guessing you meant what you said before."

She sighed. "I may have been oversimplifying."

"Look," he said as he touched her arm. "I'm not expecting a profession of love or an undying commitment. Just tell me you felt the same the draw that I did."

"I did feel something."

"That's all I ask. That you admit that you felt something."

"I don't know if it's anything, though."

"It doesn't have to be everything."

She turned up the corner of her mouth. "But just something."

He nodded. "Just a little bit of something."

"A tiny bit of something, maybe?"

He raised his eyebrow. "Tiny's not a word I want to hear."

"Little?"

"No."

"Diminutive?"

"Absolutely not."

"Pet—"

"Jake!" screamed a female voice.

Both of them froze, and he turned toward the door.

Just as a teenage girl slammed into him.

He barely caught her, but it only took him a second to realize who his attacker was.

"Child," he said, and hugged her back. He brushed her hair away from her face. "I can't…"

Emotions of joy slammed into him.

"You're alive!" she squealed. "They told me all the vampires had been killed, but I thought that was crazy because I know that you and the others would be okay, because you were smart, and you would be able to get away and make it out, but they said no one did. So I was really sad, and when Richard said we needed to come here, I didn't know why. It's been so scary! I hated it. I—"

"Slow down." Jake glanced around, looking for where she'd come from, and who she'd come in with. "What are you doing here?"

"I'm here with Sir Richard." She leaned into him, her voice going lower. "He's a huge jerk, and I can't stand him, but he's the only one who would take me after what happened. Especially now, when I need all the protection because the nasties from Europe are after me."

"Take you? What are you talking about? Who are the nasties?" Jake's voice raised as he spoke, enough that the room slowed down, and everyone turned to him.

The girl squealed. "You're all here!" And she took off after every vampire, hugging each one in turn.

Eve Harrison came over, and out of the corner of his eyes, Jake saw Megan tense.

"What's going on here?" Eve asked. "Who's the kid?"

"She was Melios's," Jake said.

"She's a vampire?" Eve asked.

"No, she isn't."

Jake turned and saw a man, in a black shirt and jeans, hair brushed out of his face, and interestingly enough, a large samurai sword on his hip.

He was pretty sure the man was a Knight Templar. Either that, or he was some kind of mythical with a sword fetish.

"Richard, dude, what's up?" Eve said. "Haven't seen you in a while. Well, not since, you know. Liam."

He gestured to the girl. "I was here to see the CEOs. I need a favor."

"What's the favor?" Eve asked.

"Her."

Eve glanced at the girl. "No. No, no, no-no-no. I'm not a fucking babysitter, Richard."

"And you're not already?" He gestured to the vampires. Including Jake.

"Excuse me?" Jake snapped.

Richard shot him a look of contempt, then turned back to Eve. "You seriously don't think this is a babysitting job, Eve?"

"I'm here working on this Cold Team for Jackstone. I'm not taking care of your wayward teen while you go pine over some damn missing person."

"Go crawl back into your hole. This isn't about you."

Eve rolled her eyes. "Fuck, it's always about me, Richard. I am who you all call whenever you need something done that's outside your lines. Well, I'm not doing it anymore. The last favor I did for you got my mate killed. So you can go fuck yourself. Take your little kid and go find a halfway house for her or something. I'm not doing *anything* for you."

Jake glanced over his shoulder at the girl, running between the vampires, all of them happy to see her. She was just as ecstatic to see them. They all clustered around her, everyone talking really fast. Jake couldn't quite hear them—what with Eve and Richard barking at each other about, well fuck, he wasn't sure what they were going on about. The past. The future. Promises and death.

Megan glanced between him and Richard and Eve, and then back at the girl.

"Who's the girl?" Megan asked.

"I thought she was dead," Jake said, marveling that the kid was here. Alive. "I thought everyone died but us."

To see the girl, it did something to him. Warmed his heart. His head. His chest.

Knowing she was alive. That she was okay. It gave him something. Something he hadn't felt in a long time.

Not in all the years he'd been with Melios, anyway.

It was different.

She was different. The girl had sort of weaved in and out of their circle at Melios's place. She was around. Sometimes a lot. Sometimes she'd just appear. Occasionally, she'd smuggle them a little extra blood behind Melios's back. In exchange, they made sure none of the vampires harmed her.

If they had a friend in the nest, it was the kid.

He shook his head.

She was alive.

He couldn't help smiling.

Eve and Richard were still barking at each other about the kid and taking care of her, neither one wanting to do it.

And it pissed Jake off.

"I'll do it."

They were going round and round, their voices getting louder.

Jake raised his. "I'll do it."

Eve must have noticed. "Huh?" She looked right at him.

Jake met her stare. "I'll. Do it."

"Do what?" Eve asked.

"I'll take care of the girl."

She shook her head. "No, you won't."

"Yes. I'll do it. You obviously don't want to. I take responsibility." He glanced at Richard. "What is the situation. How long do you need her to stay?"

"Wait. Stop. You're not in charge here," Eve said. "We don't even have room for her. She can't stay with you, she's a teenage girl. Where's she going to sleep?"

"Two weeks. Maybe a month. It depends. I have to leave the country to take care of a situation."

Jake glanced over his shoulder at the girl. "Kid, you wanna stay with me while he's gone?"

"Duh. Of course!"

"It's a done deal."

"No, it's not!" Eve put her hands on her hip.

"We'll make room, Eve," Jake said, putting his hand on her arm.

Megan cleared her throat. "There are other dormitory rooms. He could stay in one of the smaller apartments with her. It wouldn't be much to make the arrangements."

Eve wagged a finger at Megan. "You're not helping."

"I wasn't trying to."

"Big words coming from someone I could end in a flash."

Megan tossed her head back. "I've killed your kind before."

Eve raised her eyebrow. "Sure, you have, Doc. I doubt you'd even know how to."

"Decapitation works well, regardless of the species," Megan replied.

With every word Megan said, Jake knew he was going to sleep with her again.

He had to.

Was it supposed to be so sexy to watch his woman be so, well, alpha as she challenged Eve?

His desire bubbled to life in a way he'd not ever felt before.

He wanted to say it was because her calm ferocity was the sexiest thing he'd ever seen. Mix that with her hot body and the way she looked at him.

And the fact that once was never going to be enough for him when it came to Megan. He really, really wanted to fuck her.

Like a lot.

And if she kept throwing out this calm ferocity like she was doing, he may marry her.

If vampires married.

Was that a thing? He didn't know.

"Shall we go a couple rounds?" Eve said, rocking her head back and forth.

"If you are ready to be without a head," Megan said.

Jake cleared his throat. He had to do something. The hard-on blazing in his pants was killing him. "As amusing as that would be," Jake said, "Perhaps later."

"It wouldn't be amusing," Richard muttered. "It would be a waste of a good doctor."

Megan glared at him.

Richard shrugged.

"Hey, I have faith in the doc," Jake said.

Richard snorted. "You're naïve."

"You wanna go a round?" Jake asked.

Richard took a step toward Jake. "As entertaining as it would be, I really have to be going. But I promise you. We'll go a round sometime."

"Knock it off, Richard," Eve said.

Richard gestured toward the girl. "Her stuff is in the hallway."

"We're not doing this, Richard," Eve said.

Jake shook his head. "Think it's out of your hands."

"You know I could end you for this," Eve said.

"Yeah. You could," Jake said as he headed for the door.

Sure enough, out in the hall sat two suitcases. Black and white striped. Definitely belonging to a teenager.

He came back in, and Richard was walking out.

"Thanks. I'll be in touch."

"This is not over Richard. Vampires don't babysit," Eve yelled.

"This one does," Richard responded.

Eve cursed. Glared at him.

Jake didn't care.

This vampire certainly would.

17

"*Y*ou're not a big fan of Eve Harrison," Jake said to Megan.

Megan shook her head, irritated she'd lost her temper earlier. "How could you tell?"

"I had a couple of clues," Jake replied as he tucked the bedsheet. And he might have just winked at her.

"I'm not a huge fan of sheldevak."

"Why is that?"

Megan pulled on the corner of the mattress, helping Jake make up the bed in his new room across the hall from where he'd initially been staying. It was actually next door to Amy's little apartment. She might stop by and tell her what was going on.

Maybe knowing that Reynolds was in between her and the other vampires might give her some peace of mind.

"They're hard to kill, and they kill a lot of people, humans, and mythicals, to survive. I have never known one that I trusted."

"Eve seems trustable."

"Jury's still out," Megan replied. Having been with

Jackstone for quite a few years now, she'd seen a lot. She admired the company's mythical side and how they helped mythicals. It didn't matter what kind of mythical it was—werewolf, vampire, fairy, dragon, or merrow—if they were mythical and displaced, Jackstone would help.

To a point, of course.

Nothing was ever really free. It made Megan wonder what kind of favor Eve Harrison owed them to get her to do this.

"I probably should be more cautious with her." The last thing Megan wanted to do was wind up pissing off a sheldevak.

He looked at her with this sort of sideways smile. Not showing teeth, but just kind of arrogant and knowing, but also a little bit of understanding. "I bet you could take her."

She smiled. "I bluff really well," she said as she glanced at him. Again. Because he was still really cute. He could have been in a movie, he was so sexy.

It sucked how much her mind thought back to him all day.

She wasn't going to come down to his gym and talk to him. She didn't want to start anything more with him.

Yet she couldn't help it. She had to see him. She owed him something, anyway.

Something had been enough. But was it enough for her? That she didn't know. That was the damn problem.

"I don't think you were bluffing."

Lord, his voice sent all sorts of vibes through her. In all the good ways.

He gave her a sly grin.

And she felt it again. She wanted to kick her own ass.

It was just a smile. A guy vampire smile.

Focus on the task.

"No. I've never taken down a sheldevak."

"Could have fooled me."

She shrugged. "She's right, it's not common for a werewolf to take out a sheldevak. Usually, only Alphas can do that."

"Why?"

"They're stronger."

He nodded. "So your pack, are they strong? That's the right word, right? Pack?"

She nodded. "Yes. And no. I don't have a pack. Not anymore."

"Something happen to them?"

"They died."

"I'm sorry."

"I am too. Sheldevak killed them. Some kind of fight. So, when you ask, no, I'm not a fan of her species. Her, I don't have an opinion on, one way or the other. However, she's a bit more arrogant than others I've met."

"I'm sorry."

"You didn't do it." Unfortunately, she could still see those who did. The way they popped in and out of existence, monster shadows that appeared and disappeared. They could kill anyone, any time.

As long as they saw where they were going, or so she'd been told.

She flipped out the bedspread, sending it flying over the full-sized bed, almost entirely in place.

"Magic," Jake whispered.

Megan glanced at him. "What?"

He shook his head. "Sorry. My mom. She used to say 'magic' when she fluffed the bedspread out. Something about me being a kid. I thought it was magical, how she could make it float in the air."

She grinned. And her eyes got surprisingly wet. She could imagine a little boy next to a bed, watching his mother fluff out a blanket, and being mesmerized by the floating linen.

And the image was exactly what she needed, so she wasn't wallowing about her family.

"That was a sweet story. Thank you for sharing it with me." She smoothed the bedspread into place.

"Welcome," he said as he helped straighten it and put the pillow in place. "I haven't thought about my mother in a long time."

"Does she know? About your current state?"

He shook his head. "She died when I was in high school. Part of the reason I went into the military. Didn't have anything else to do after school. Both parents were gone. No siblings around."

"You were looking for a family."

"I was looking for a purpose." He glanced around the room. "And look at me now."

She walked around the bed toward him. "Look at you. Alive. Safe. Warm. In free temporary housing."

"Just as lost."

"Not for long," she said and put her hand on his arm, his skin cool to the touch.

He met her gaze, his eyes the pale gray color of vampires. Pale gray, but a touch of green in them. Just a little bit more than she'd noticed before.

He returned her touch, his hand chilly against her skin. "I hope you're right."

They looked at each other for a moment.

Maybe a moment too long. Megan felt those tingles of flirtation, of desire one felt when they looked at each other.

She wasn't going to kiss him.

No. She wasn't.

The nightmares didn't mean anything. She wouldn't consider anything else. He couldn't possibly be her mate. It didn't matter that werewolves had those nightmares. It was her wolf, trying to tell her about meeting Jake.

That's all.

It couldn't be more.

Could it?

"Megan," he whispered, his breath warm across her face.

"Jake, I,"

He leaned down, and just barely brushed his lips against hers. Her desires kicked up, but it wasn't that crazed, have-to-screw desire, this was something else.

A slow boil.

She pulled away before it became more.

Instead, she turned her attention to the other bedroom across the hallway, where the teenager had taken over.

This dormitory had two dinky bedrooms, but they had the basics that Jake and the kid would need to live for a short time, while the girl was staying with them.

She was putting put away her things like she was moving in permanently.

And was she humming to herself?

Such a strange situation. Who was this girl? What did the vampires know about her? Was she a vampire? Something else? If she was a born-vampire or born-any kind of mythical, really, the mythical side didn't usually present until the child was mid-teen. Not that there weren't 9-year-old werewolves running around. A kid who had werewolf parents, and saw their parents shift, was more likely to shift early. She treated a boy just last week—while in wolf form, he sliced up his leg really bad.

Regardless, something tended to present.

But the girl, though.

She didn't seem to have any signs of a mythical at all. Megan wasn't sure what to think. The teen seemed normal enough. But the doctor had seen plenty of mythicals who *seemed* normal enough at first.

She never did catch the girl's name.

"What is her name?" she asked, gesturing to the girl's room.

Jake shrugged.

Megan stared at him, aghast. "Do you not know?"

He shook his head. "Nope, I don't. She was always Kid. Or Child."

Megan blinked. "You're kidding."

"No. I never heard her called anything but Child or Kid." He laid some personal items on the dresser. "Never called her anything else."

"You didn't ask?"

Megan pivoted on her heel and walked out. That was just insane. Everyone had a name.

She stopped in the doorway. The girl was dancing about, humming to herself, lost in her own little world.

Megan knocked on the doorway.

She froze, and her gaze snapped around and hit Megan. Her eyes were so cold and stark, if the look had been physical, it would have knocked her down.

"Hi," she said, smiling at her. "You know, honey, I never caught your name. I'm Megan, by the way."

"Okay. Megan."

"What's your name, sweetie?"

She blinked. "I don't have one."

"Well, everyone has a name."

"I don't."

"Well, how do you know when people are talking to you?"

"I just do."

"Surely you have a name of some kind. It helps you identify yourself. You know who you are."

"I don't know who I am." She shrugged, like what she said was no big thing.

Megan's heart went out to the girl. The child was serious. She didn't have a name.

She felt a tear well up in her eyes again. To not know who, or what, she was. That felt like its own special kind of torture.

Regardless of Megan's unconventional life, she always knew she was a werewolf. She always knew there were certain things she had to do to take care of herself. If there was one thing her pack instilled, it was the importance of knowing how to handle the mythical side.

"Maybe you should think of one," Jake said from the doorway.

Megan glanced back at him.

How had she not noticed him come up behind her?

His shoulder bumped hers. He glanced at her, and Megan couldn't help looking at his light eyes for just a moment too long.

That warmth. That comfort. It hit her every time he came near. She wasn't afraid of him. That's why she didn't register he was there. She was that comfortable around him. That bothered her.

A great deal.

Maybe more than the girl without a name.

The girl cleared her throat, her intense gaze seeming so tangible, it dug into her. Into them actually, so much. The girl blinked very slowly and deliberately, and Megan was struck by how violet her eyes were. Not gray. Not blue, but violet.

Quite beautiful, if the color didn't give her such a strange vibe. There was something not quite right about it.

Like she knew things. Things no teenager should, and Megan couldn't help wondering what the kid had been through.

She would be hitting her medical journals and mythical lore when she got home, to see if she could figure out about the girl's eye color. Something stabbed at her about it—like it was on the tip of her tongue, but she couldn't remember.

"I'll think about a name," the girl finally said.

"Pick whatever you want, Kid."

"What if I want Kid?"

"Then it's yours," Jake said.

She nodded. Her gaze danced around the room before landing back on Megan and Jake.

"So when do we eat? I'm hungry."

Megan smiled. "Now that sounds like a teenager."

18

"So, what's going on, Kid?" Jake asked the girl after they got settled. Megan had left already. Something about bonding time, she'd said. He wished she was still here.

He liked having the doctor around—because he liked her. A lot. And because, well, she was a doctor. She might be able to help with the kid.

Once he figured out what exactly was happening with her. He hadn't said anything to the kid until now, but he knew something serious had to be going on if she needed protecting. She was a teenager. It wasn't like she couldn't be left alone for a while. And didn't he read that the Templars had some big compound or something? Some kind of base, anyway.

Why would she need to be removed from that?

The girl chewed on her burger. Looked off into the distance.

"Kid."

"Evelyn," she said.

"What's Evelyn?"

"Me. I like Evelyn."

Jake nodded. "Well, okay then. You can be Evelyn." Not exactly what he wanted to talk about, but if it segued into what was a bit more important, he'd talk about it. Because he needed to know what he was up against.

She smiled. "If I knew picking a name was that easy, I would have done it a long time ago."

Jake nodded. "Most people don't pick their names. They are usually given them by their parents."

"Huh," she said. Chewed another bite of her hamburger. A corner of the meat fell off the burger.

The smell of the meat made Jake's mouth water, just a bit. But it was more of a memory, a long-lost desire to really enjoy a good burger. Or a steak. Or some ribs.

Meat. Jake loved meat. He missed eating meat. Hence the life of being an immortal vampire. He could drink stuff—wine, coffee, tea, soda, all that if he wanted. Just no solids.

Made a meat lover like him wonder how rude it would be to lick a steak.

Maybe he would try it. Next time he had a—

"They've been coming for me," she—Evelyn—finally said.

He glanced at her, drawn out of his plans of cheating to get meat flavor. "Who has?"

She shrugged.

"Who are they?"

She shrugged again.

"Why do they want you?"

"I don't know," she said, her voice raised a bit.

He looked at her. The soldier in him immediately started determining scenarios and writing out potential outcomes. But he didn't know all the facts and trying to understand why a Knight Templar brought her here, just didn't make sense.

Unless he was trying to hide her.

And if so, then why were they hiding her? Who was after her? The Templars were supposed to be these big bad-assed dudes, according to the books Eve had been forcing them to study.

But who was coming if the Templars were afraid? And what did that mean for Jake and the others?

Not enough facts yet.

Something about the way she was looking off into space —it was deliberate. Deceitful, in a way. Like she was hiding things.

"Look at me."

Her gaze cut to him; her eyes were cold. Distant. Void of emotion.

"Why are they after you, Evelyn?"

"Because I killed Melios. His family is pissed off." Her words were just as cold and distant. Like she gave zero fucks about what the problem was.

"That would do it," Jake said, keeping his tone neutral, though inside he was freaking out.

He shook his head.

Stunned. Flabbergasted.

This kid. This teenaged kid killed Melios. He was one of the most powerful vampires on the planet, or so he professed. Who knew how many years he had been around? Or centuries for that matter.

Someone who'd stayed alive for a very long time had been taken down by a teen.

Jake looked her up and down.

She shrugged. "He was distracted. I just did what you taught me. Right through the heart. He never saw it coming."

She didn't seem to care about what she'd done.

It gave him a shiver.

"Why?" As far as Jake knew, she considered Melios a kind of father. She behaved as such, anyway. They'd argue. Then they'd be friends again. Hell, at first Jake thought the girl was Melios's child. He'd classified their relationship as tumultuous, but not more than that. Not any more than a young teen and a parent.

She shrugged again.

Jake raised his eyebrow. "Why would you do that, kid?"

The cold look in her eyes from before turned fiery hot as she screamed at him. "Do you really want him back?"

Jake shook his head. "Of course not."

She brushed a strand of her dirty blond hair out of her face. "Then, I was doing the world a favor. He was a monster."

"I won't disagree with you, kid. But why now?"

"Opportunity," she said. She took another bite of her burger. "So, can I go stream a movie or something?"

Jake blinked, stunned by the sudden shift in her personality. "Sure."

"Cool," she said, grinning, and she got up, leaving the burger half-eaten on the table. "And now I can finally get back to a normal sleeping schedule."

He raised his eyebrow. "Normal?"

She grinned. "I'm a night person." And she bounced to the couch and started up the streaming service.

Jake picked up her remaining burger and looked at it.

"This is going to be interesting," he muttered.

"Rise and shine, my little sunspots!"

Loud banging on Jake's door made him bolt upright.

He reached for a weapon, but there wasn't one there.

He glanced around. Reoriented.

Took him a second to untangle himself from the kid. Evelyn. They'd fallen asleep watching movies. She hadn't wanted to be alone in a new place. He got that. So they marathoned something.

He didn't remember what.

And now, that damn sheldevak woman was banging on his door.

"Get up, Reynolds!"

He got up and crossed to the door, and probably would have opened it to let her in, but she just appeared in his living room.

"Do you not bother with doors?"

"Not when I don't have to." She tipped her head to the side, looking at Evelyn.

"Problem?"

"No." She met his gaze. "Get your team up and ready in twenty. We got a job."

Jake nodded.

A job.

Great.

Evelyn yawned on the couch and stretched.

"What am I going to do with her?" he muttered.

"Not my fucking problem," Eve replied. "You're the one who wanted to babysit. You deal with it."

He glared at her.

"Eighteen minutes."

Jake ran his hand over his head.

Shit.

19

*M*egan yanked open her door.

It would have been much more dramatic if Jake Reynolds hadn't just pushed through, looking disheveled and steamy, towing the teenaged girl with him.

"Need your help," he panted.

She glanced at him, because, well looking at him was always a treat. But also, because he seemed to be literally smoking.

Megan glanced behind him and realized the sun was still going down.

She raised her eyebrow. "What are you doing out in the sunlight? You do know you're a vampire, and can't be out in the sunshine, right? It will burn you up."

He glowered at her. "I'm not an idiot."

She tipped her head to the side. "I wonder about that when I see you out in daylight."

He huffed. And probably didn't mean to swirl the steamy smoke coming off him around, but he did, and it was kinda funny.

Or kinda sexy.

She kinda wanted to see how long he'd steam. And if all of him was steaming. And wouldn't that be fun if he was?

Gah!

"What's going on?" she asked, brushing past the thoughts she wasn't supposed to be having about a damn vampire. She knew better than this, but it seemed like whenever she was around him, she went a little bonkers.

Amazing sex will do that to a person.

"I need a favor."

"Uh-huh." *Keep it professional*, she told herself as she pulled out her backup medical bag from the hall closet. He stood there, awkwardly, while she started digging around. Surely, she had something in there for almost toasty vampires.

Though it was looking like some Fairy Tea may be her only option here at home. She didn't keep bags of blood on hand at the house.

"Oh, it's you," the teen said, crossed her arms and pouted. "Didn't realize *you* were who he was talking about."

"Be nice." Jake glared at the girl. "Listen, she'll keep you safe for a few hours while I go do this. It won't be very long. You'll be okay here."

"Wait, what?"

"Watch the kid."

"Ugh." The kid flipped her hair. "Evelyn," she said with the kind of disrespect only a teenager could have.

"Evelyn. Sorry." Jake said, looking at her, then turned back to Megan. "Please watch Evelyn for a couple of hours. We have a job to do, and I can't take her with me." He looked at Megan with a pleading expression.

"You probably could have," Evelyn muttered. "It's not like I wasn't trained to fight."

"That's not the point." Jake glowered at her. "There are reasons you can't be alone right now."

The girl huffed.

153

Megan waved her hand. "First off, what the hell gives you the right to just barge into my house and ask a favor. Second, what if I wasn't available? I could have a date. A second job. I could have been *with someone*."

The girl snorted.

"No, you wouldn't have been." Jake's eyes went dark. Not in a sexy way, either.

"Don't even," Megan countered to Jake, pointing at him. "You don't get to tell me what to do. I'm not your soldier."

He stepped closer to her. "You like it when I tell you what to do."

"It seems I was giving the orders."

He raised his eyebrow. "Maybe I let you."

"You two are gross," the girl said.

Megan sighed and turned back to Jake. "And third, why do you even know where I live?"

"That one was me," the girl said. "I hacked the computer."

Megan raised her eyebrow. "You hacked the Jackstone computers?"

"Like it's hard," she said with a massive eye roll.

"Please, Megan, I need this. She just wants to stream more of her show. What is it? The Desperate Housewives thing?"

"So, that's probably not kid-appropriate," Megan said.

"I'm fifteen. I'm not a child."

Megan had so many familial moments flash in her mind, like the same argument with her own mother. And it took everything to not spout off the sarcastic comment her own mother used to say back to her.

Megan ignored her attitude. "I see you chose a name."

"It'll do. For now."

Megan nodded. "Evelyn. Sounds very sophisticated." It was an excellent choice.

She shrugged. "Whatever. Where's your TV?"

"In there," Megan said, gesturing to her family room.

As soon as the girl got out of earshot, Megan grabbed Jake's arm. "What the hell were you thinking? I can't keep her! She doesn't know me. I don't know her. It's rude. And unsafe. I could be a monster."

"You're not," Jake replied.

"I could be!"

"Jake! This is such a bad idea." She glanced back at the girl who didn't look like she was streaming any Desperate Housewife thing at all. Looked more like it was a cartoon. Anime maybe?

"I can't leave her alone." He leaned in with his voice low. "She killed my sire, and now his clan is coming after her. That's why the Templars had to hide her. For her safety."

"What?" Megan glanced toward the room, where the girl was zooming through the streaming channel's selection. "That child--and I don't care what she says, she's still a kid-- that's about to watch a cartoon, is the one who killed your sire? Wasn't he supposed to have been centuries old?"

Jake nodded.

Her mind danced in a thousand directions. Questions that didn't make any sense. Like at all. "I can't. What? It—"

"I know. It's crazy. I've been trying to wrap my mind around it myself. And now we have a job to do for Jackstone. If I screw it up, I may not be here tomorrow. Then she'd really be hosed."

Megan sighed. "Fine. For tonight. That's it, though. Like that's totally it. So you'd better not die."

"Not planning on it." Jake nodded. "Thank you." He leaned down and kissed her cheek.

It was quick.

Chaste.

And it was so much more than that.

She might have melted just a bit, standing there.

He was gone before she came out of her haze.

"Damn, that man."

"REALLY? YOU WAKE UP NAKED?" Evelyn was staring at Megan, her jaw agape. "And you like, don't even know where you were?"

Megan shrugged and tossed some popcorn in her mouth. She nodded while she chewed the bite. "Yep, one of the scary parts of being a werewolf."

"Especially a girl werewolf," Evelyn added.

"You have no idea," she said.

Her eyes got wide. "What happened?"

Megan shrugged, unsure if she should tell this girl all her horrible secrets from her youth. But they were bonding. And Megan was pretty sure, just from the little bit she knew about Melios, that this girl probably didn't have a healthy bonding experience with anyone in her life.

"Let's just say that some human boys will not mess with a woman ever again." She waggled her eyebrows.

Evelyn's eyes got wide. "Do I want to know what you did to them?"

She held up her hands. "I didn't touch them. They made the mistake of touching me."

Evelyn grinned. "Boys should know better than to touch girls."

"Most do," she answered, and picked up her drink.

The girl picked up her own and started running her finger around the top of the glass. It was an absentminded motion the girl made, like someone trying to play a water glass.

Megan waited to hear the sound, that high-pitched resonance that she'd likely hear before the girl realized she was doing it.

But she didn't hear the usual sound she expected to hear. Instead, she heard a hum that she didn't recognize.

She blinked.

"What?" The girl asked. Her finger stopped. "What's the matter?"

The humming stopped.

Megan gestured to the girl's hand. "I heard your, uh, gesture."

"You heard it? You hear that well?"

"I'm part wolf, honey. I hear a lot when I open up my senses."

'That would be a cool trait to have," she said and started circling the cup again. "I don't know what cool traits I have."

"Well, I am a doctor. Tell me your lineage, and I can tell you what to expect."

"I don't know what I am," she said.

"Well, who were your parents?"

"I don't know," she said. It wasn't said with any sort of emotion, just that she didn't know. "Melios always said I was special. But I don't know why." She kept running her finger around the edge of the glass.

Megan tipped her head to the side and appraised her. "At first look, I would think you were a human-vampire mix, because of your pale skin. Your eyes though are different. If you were a vampire, it would show in your eyes."

She nodded. "I know. Everyone had light, shiny eyes. Mine aren't like that."

"We could always take some blood and see what comes back. In fact, I think there's a genetics department on Avalon. I'm sure they could track your DNA back to figure out exactly what you are."

"Avalon?" she asked.

Megan blinked. "You don't know about Avalon?"

She shook her head. "Like Avalon, from King Arthur?"

"Yes and no. Avalon is a magically shielded island off the coast of the United Kingdom. Lots of mythicals live there."

"Magically shielded? Still, someone would have found it by now, surely."

"The island moves."

"Wow," she said. "How do you know so much about it?"

"I'm a doctor. I did a semester of mythical study there. A lot of doctors who want to treat mythicals go to Avalon, for a semester at least, and study. There's no greater concentration or variation of mythicals on the planet. Except for here."

She nodded. "Melios said once, something about here being a great place to build his army. Is there something here that attracts them?" She kept making the motion with her hand.

But her hand had lifted from the glass.

And the liquid was still moving.

"Evelyn," Megan said. "How are you doing that?"

The girl looked down. She pulled her hand back, and the water, like it was on a leash, followed the gesture.

The liquid came up, out of the glass and splashed on Evelyn.

Both of them squealed.

Leaped off the couch.

"What was that?" Megan asked, gesturing to the now empty cup.

"I—I don't know. It's never done that before," she said, shaking her head. Her eyes were wide, and she looked terrified. "I've stirred the water, but not pulled it out of the glass before!"

Megan headed into the kitchen to get some towels. And started running through every mythical she could think of, that could do what that girl did. While she didn't have any apparent signs, she could have some water-based lineage, like some merrow blood or siren or something.

Immediately, Megan's brain went into overdrive, categorizing mythicals, and trying to remember which ones could manipulate water. What was this girl, anyway?

"It's pretty cool," Megan said as she came back.

Distress marred Evelyn's face as she patted on the couch, trying to wipe up the bit of liquid.

"It's fine," Megan said as she started sopping things up with the towels. "Can you do that on command? Like, move the water?"

She shrugged again. "Never really thought about it."

"Maybe you could hone it, somehow?"

"Maybe." They got the water cleaned up, and Megan picked up the wet paper towels to throw them away.

When the hairs on her neck stood up.

She turned.

Looked toward her front door.

"What, what is it?"

"I smell something," Megan said. And she did.

She wasn't sure exactly what it was at first, but it was out there. She took a couple of steps toward the door. She could feel the energy outside. A deep breath and she could smell them.

Him.

It was one mythical. One man.

A strong smell of heat. Fire. Burning.

Oh hell.

She inched toward the door and looked outside. There was only one mythical she could think of off the top of her head that smelled like that.

What the hell was a dragon doing outside? What the hell was a dragon doing this far south of the Arctic?

Megan glanced back at the girl. She'd stood up, her face somber, and suddenly she looked much older.

"They're coming," she said.

"We don't have much time," Megan said, rocking her neck. Because she already knew, this wasn't going to be pretty. "We need to get out of here." She was a werewolf, but she wasn't a massively *strong* werewolf.

Though she could fight. She'd done it before.

She would do it again.

Megan grabbed her medical bag from the closet and pulled out a couple of disposable rain ponchos, the kind one got for a dollar. She looked back at the girl.

"It's going to get very interesting, very, very quickly, Evelyn." There were questions because, of course, there were questions—like how the hell did the dragon get here? He must have been watching, but if he was, then why attack here and not at Jackstone? Why wait until they were inside? Why not attack when she'd been dropped off when Jake was most vulnerable?

The girl nodded.

Megan pushed the bag toward her. "Carry this. The back door is through the kitchen. Head back that way now." Her werewolf was dancing inside, ready to burst out.

Ready to fight.

"Okay."

She touched the girl's arm, and their eyes locked. "Trust my wolf, Evelyn. I may not be able to speak, but I'm a helluva survivor."

The wolf growled under her skin.

She might have let out some of the noise.

"Someday I might like to hear those stories," Evelyn replied.

"Hopefully someday they'll just be stories," Megan answered. Her human anger flared. She was a goddamn doctor. She wasn't a warrior. She went into medicine to heal people.

There wasn't supposed to be this shit anymore. And yet, here she was, going back to that primal side.

The side she'd tried to control, all her life.

That fucking side was going to save her.

Damn.

She waved the teen back. "Go, get back there."

The smell got stronger toward the front of the house.

Megan pulled off her tank and her leggings and tossed them on the couch. No point in destroying them if she didn't have to. Her human side, trying to maintain some kind of control.

But the beast wasn't having it.

The wolf rolled around inside her, ready. Desperate for the attack.

Wait.

Just wait.

The smell got stronger.

Now.

20

*W*atching Megan transform was quite a sight to see.

Evelyn had never been around many werewolves. Seeing how the hair just sort of flew out of her skin, the bones popped and cracked, and yet it was so fast, it was almost like a magic trick.

It kind of was.

A twist in her gut, the idea that had been shoved down her throat—that werewolves were enemies and needed to be destroyed—gnawed at her. Melios had spent a lot of time drilling that into her, and even now, she had to remind herself this was Dr. Megan. Not some random beast she should fight against.

Evelyn hugged the bag she'd been given, plus her own purse she'd thought to grab as she headed for the back door.

As the wolf hit the ground, it glanced back at her for a second, then headed toward the front door.

Too bad.

The wolf might have seen the guy come in the window.

Evelyn rolled her eyes. Maybe they were stupid like

Melios had always said. Too bad. She'd had hopes that Melios had been wrong about everything.

So far, though, it wasn't looking like he was.

The attacker burst in through the window, practically melting the glass.

The dragon's body head poured off him like a tangible river. He wasn't really focusing on Megan, the wolf. Instead, he headed straight for her. Two candles melted on the table, the wax just oozing down into piles of goo as he walked through the house. He radiated heat, and Evelyn felt herself begin to sweat.

When Melios had been dealing with dragons, they'd always been hot, but this one was molten, almost. His skin kind of glowed, even.

She might have been fascinated if he didn't look like he was ready to rip her apart.

She crept back toward the kitchen, watching.

Wolf attacked.

Slams.

Hits.

Growls.

Flames erupted.

The dragon hissed at the wolf, and the heat set the table on fire. The wolf lunged at the dragon.

Back and forth they went.

Evelyn pulled out her phone and texted Jake. Not that she thought he could do anything, but she sent him a short, sweet text.

A dragon. Here. Now. - Evelyn

Maybe that'll get his attention. She didn't know what Jake and the others were up to, other than they had some kind of mission tonight, but be back in a few hours—or so he'd said.

She'd been pissed off when Jake dumped her on the doctor lady, but she seemed kind enough. She probably could have tolerated her for the night.

She might have even played around with the water thing.

You know, just because.

A bitter smell hit Evelyn, and she could see where some of Megan's fur was burnt. "Ouch," she muttered.

The dragon looked her way.

Shit, she thought. Evelyn backed up until she hit the sink.

The dragon threw the wolf across the room. His skin partially morphing into scales, the heat like fire-hot trim outlining the scales.

Evelyn reached behind her and found the sink's hose. She pulled the sprayer out and shot water at him.

It didn't quite reach. At least not at first.

"Go!" she shouted at the water. Almost like she blew it, kinda like that superhero in that tv show she'd been watching. The water shifted and headed straight for the dragon.

Whoa. That could be fun to figure out, later.

Now was not the time, though.

The dragon got closer.

She shot more water.

Steam flew off him, hissing.

"Shit," she muttered and tried to run away in the flash steam.

The dragon, however, kept up.

"You get away from me," she said.

"What are you going to do to me?" A fire glowed all around the dragon.

She shot more water at him.

He steamed.

She took off.

He reached out and grabbed her arm.

Evelyn cried out, dropping her bags. "Let go of me! Do you know who I am?" Smoke and fog filled the house. Everything around her was burning.

The world was burning.

And Megan was laying on the floor in the living room. Would she be okay?

"You can't do this to me," she spat at him, wincing from the burns on her arm.

"Yes, I can." The dragon kept a hold of her and dragged her outside.

As soon as they made it into the back yard, the dragon shot flames at the house, setting it fully on fire.

Wings popped out of his shoulders.

"Hold on," he said.

"You're burning me."

"Be thankful that's the only thing I'm doing to you." The wings spread out, and he rolled his shoulders. The wings moved.

And they launched from the ground into the air.

21

"*L*isten, you do not run out on a job, I don't give a fuck who it is or what is going on," Eve Harrison bellowed at Jake, her hand on the oh-shit handle in the passenger seat.

Jake growled.

"I'm not kidding," Eve said. "I will fucking end you."

"You haven't done it yet," he replied.

He gave zero fucks about it. Pulling his team off a job went against everything he'd ever been taught in the military.

He wasn't screwing around.

"Dragon," Jake said.

She blinked. "Are you sure?"

He glanced at her. Then back at the road. The kid had said dragon. He'd only fought a dragon once, and he didn't do well. At the time, he wondered if he'd heal at all. He didn't want to face another one if he could help it.

He kept driving. Desperation and panic fueled his speeding through Liverly streets until he came to Megan's neighborhood.

Mythical or not, she wouldn't be able to handle a dragon.

Not alone. It would be like trying to fight a bomb with a baby rattle.

Please.

Please be okay...

"No answer," Joanie said. "Still."

Jake grimaced. He'd had Joanie start texting the kid ever since they got in the car, trying to find out more info.

He rounded the corner.

The house—Megan's home—was engulfed in flames.

"Holy fucking hell," Eve Harrison said. "Please tell me that's not Doc's house."

"It is," Jake said. He barely got the car pulled over. Years of training ran through his mind, a thousand tactical approaches hit him, and he started figuring the best way to get to the house, unseen.

Because vampires couldn't be seen. He had to come in from the side, out of the way. His adrenalin pumped, or whatever the fuck it was now that he was a vampire, and he felt his fangs elongate.

He let out a breath. The monster was coming out to play.

Eve grabbed his arm before he leaped out. She met his gaze and nodded. "I'll distract them. You do what you have to."

She glanced at the others. "Malcomb, Thompson, you two back him up. Collins and Alekhine, you're with me."

Jake glanced back. Malcomb and Thompson put their game faces on—fangs out, and ready to fight.

Joanie and Travis went with Eve.

They got out, and Eve stumbled up to the nearest line of firemen, babbling almost incoherently about her friend's house, and where was the owner, how it was her friend. Collins and Alekhine followed, Joanie comforting Eve, Collins rounding out the distraction, being an irate relative.

Pretty darn convincing performance.

Jake leaped into the dark, night air, out of sight of the flashing lights of the first responders.

Well, what do you know, he could leap tall buildings—or at least neighborhood houses—in a single bound.

He landed on the roof next to Megan's home, looking through the burning building for any sign of Megan and Evelyn. Thompson and Malcomb landed next to him.

"There," Malcomb whispered. Something shined in the back yard.

He focused on it.

The shine from a cell phone.

And there, what was that?

"Fuck," Thompson whispered.

Megan was naked, covered in soot, lying in her backyard.

Jake leaped down there. The firemen either hadn't seen her or she only just emerged from the building. He wasn't taking any chances, he had to get her away.

She had her hand on a bag.

Wasn't that the same bag she'd had before? Whatever it was, she obviously thought it was necessary, she had her hand on it. He scooped it up as well as the cell phone and the other smaller bag.

That was Evelyn's. He recognized the striping on it.

Shit.

Where was Evelyn?

"Where is she?" Malcomb whispered, just as he landed next to him. He and Thompson started moving around the back yard, staying in the shadows as best they could, but still, looking for other signs of Evelyn.

"Look," Thompson said, gesturing to the ground.

Malcomb ran his foot over the ground.

A large circle of burnt grass. In the dark, hardly noticeable. Come dawn, it'll be easy to see. Megan half-laid on it.

Shit.

Jake recognized the dragon markings. Burn spots where they take flight. Damn.

The dragon could be anywhere now.

He pulled Megan close to him, cradling her in his arms. Jake had to get her out of there before they were caught by the humans.

He heard voices in the distance, and it sounded like they were coming closer.

With Megan in his arms, he leaped into the yard next door. He hit the ground harder than he wanted, tumbling forward, and almost dropping her.

Almost.

He put his hand on Megan's face, trying to wake her up. "Come on, Megan. Wake up for me, girl."

Megan coughed.

He kept his hand on her face. "Where's Evelyn?"

"Dragon took her," Megan croaked out.

"Alive?"

Megan nodded.

He held her against him.

"Let's get you out of here."

TWENTY MINUTES LATER, Megan was the one in the hospital bed, with a team of five vampires and a sheldevak around her bed.

Guards to protect her.

The only person they let in between them was Amy, the nurse. Even the on-call doctor had not been welcomed at first.

Though every one of them trusted Amy. Maybe it was

guilt over what Deke tried to do to her. Or maybe she just had that trustworthy appearance.

Didn't matter. She was allowed inside the circle whenever she needed.

Like now.

She tapped Malcomb on the shoulder. "Excuse me," she said.

Malcomb glanced at her. "Sure." She came through the sort of wall, and saw to Megan, adjusting the oxygen.

"She's going to be alright," Amy said. "But I need to wash her up," she said, and her gaze landed on Jake. "If you don't mind."

Jake blinked.

And then glanced at the others. "Right."

Realizing she wanted them to leave the room.

Eve Harrison had been on her phone texting furiously at someone.

"Everyone out," she said. "Alekhine, stay in here with her. Someone needs to be in here with her. Just in case."

Joanie nodded. "I got her."

The boys walked out into the hallway, and Eve led them away from the room.

Eve put her hand on Jake's arm. "She's going to be fine. A little smoke inhalation, but she's okay. She'll be fine tomorrow."

"I know," he said. He glanced back at the room, where the nurse and Joanie were adjusting the covers to allow them to tend more to Megan.

He turned away. "I just want to find the bastard that did this."

"That will be the trick, I think," Eve said. She gestured for them to follow her. "We need a little privacy of our own."

"What do you know?" Jake asked.

She met his gaze. "It's not good."

22

*E*ve found them a small waiting room for visitors at the hospital, just down the hall from Megan's room. She glanced around and grimaced.

"What's going on?" Malcomb asked.

She held up a finger to shush him. "Everyone sit down and look defeated."

"Won't be hard," Malcomb muttered.

She pulled out a little device from her pocket, the size of a cell phone, but it looked like a garage door opener.

She clicked the button, held it for a few seconds, then double-tapped it.

A small green light blinked on it.

Jake felt a weird wave sort of move through him. "What was that?"

"Blocking field. Prevents anything from recording what we actually say. It sends back a faked image that loops any security that might be recording in this room, which is why I had you all sit still for a moment."

"Clever," Thompson said.

"It is what it is." She tossed her head back and glared at

them all. "Now. This thing only lasts about five minutes. Here's what I know."

"How do you *know* anything?" Jake asked, glaring at her.

"Did you think I was on social media back there in that hospital room?" She tipped her head back. "I saw you glaring at me."

He blinked. If anything, her playing on her phone had annoyed him more than anything, because he assumed the worst. He'd assumed she wasn't actually trying to track stuff down but playing.

"He always does that," Malcomb said.

"Fuck off," Jake snapped. He turned to Eve. "It better be worth it."

"Relax Reynolds. It is"

He crossed his arms. All the bolstering wasn't going to get him anywhere. He needed to find Evelyn as soon as possible.

While there still was a 'possible.'

"Okay short version. Templars brought the kid here because they've already had armies of mythicals looking for this girl."

"Evelyn."

"She does have a name?" Eve asked.

"She does," Jake said.

"Evelyn then. Whatever. Point is, mythicals want her head on a platter. They've attacked the Templar compound twice already."

"Who's attacking them? And why?" Malcomb asked.

"They think it's Melios's family," Eve said.

"That's what Evelyn said," Jake muttered, remembering their conversation before.

"Why?" Thompson asked.

"I didn't know he had any more family," Collins said. "He never talked about it, that I remember. Except for his dead sister."

"Oh, he has a family," Eve said. "A big one."

"And they're pissed Evelyn killed Melios," Jake muttered.

Everyone in the room turned to him.

"What?" everyone, except Eve, said at the same time.

"Evelyn. Killed. Melios." Jake made sure he spoke clearly. Because even saying it out loud, it didn't seem real. They all knew Melios was dead, but to think the kid did it? That she took him out?

It had blindsided him before. Now, it still seemed far-fetched.

Even Eve Harrison looked impressed. "How do you know that?"

"She told me."

"And you believed her?" Eve said.

Jake nodded. "No reason not to."

"Other than she's been shuffled from place to place all her life with no loyalty to anyone except maybe a psychopathic vampire, so no, I don't know why you wouldn't question her." Eve rolled her eyes.

"The kid's had it hard, but she's never lied to me," Jake said.

"That you know of," Collins added.

Jake glared at him.

Collins shrugged. "I'm just saying it. She was truthful to you because it served a purpose. If lying about killing Melios served a purpose, she'd do that too. We all know that Melios used whatever was necessary to get what he wanted. Doesn't it stand to reason the kid's going to follow suit?"

"What purpose would it serve to lie about that?"

"Lots of reasons," Thompson said.

"Trying to make herself look tough."

"Set us up for something," Malcomb added.

Jake raised his eyebrow. "Why would she be doing that?"

Malcomb shrugged. "They have a point. While I'm glad

the kid's alive, I wouldn't put it past her to do whatever she had to, to survive."

"Like us," Jake said.

He nodded. "Like us."

"We've only got a minute," Eve said. "If a dragon took the kid, then it was doing it on contract. Dragons don't give a crap about vampires. Never have."

"Contract? Like for hire?" Collins asked.

Eve nodded. "He was probably hired for housekeeping."

"Lovely fucking name for contract killers."

The tension crackled between them all for a few seconds.

Leave it to Malcomb to break through the silence. "So, what do we do now, oh, great leader?"

"I think you talk to me and ask me what happened," Dr. Criger said from the doorway.

23

"*I* really don't think you should be up, doctor," Amy said, glaring at Megan as she slipped a hand under her arm to steady her.

Megan waved her hand. "I'm fine," she said, trying to pull away.

But Amy wasn't letting go.

"Is this payback?" Megan whispered.

"Not even close," Amy said with a smile. "Did you know those damn seaweed wrap thingies tingle? Like all the time?"

"You're better, though," Megan replied.

"Maybe, but now you get to drink all the Fairy Tea."

"At least I will," Megan replied. "It's already working." Amy had given her some tea almost immediately upon arrival at the hospital, and like the stuff does, it started working, and already Megan felt far better than she should for what she'd been through tonight.

"You sure you're supposed to be up?" Jake Reynolds asked, his light eyes marred with worry.

It was kinda cute, the expression on his face.

But not completely cute. He looked irritated. Like he

wanted to put her back in bed. And not in the sexy, adult way she'd like him to do.

Damn.

There she went again.

Focus on the moment. Not on Jake.

"I'm not going to be running any marathons, but I'm not too bad," Megan said. And really, she wasn't.

It was amazing what Fairy Tea could do for a mythical. While most of the time, human medicines worked well for her, this time, since she'd been in her wolf form when she'd gotten the most damage, the magical tea did more for her.

And already she was feeling like herself.

Mostly.

And then she coughed and winced from the pain. Everything got fuzzy for a second, and the next thing she knew, she was floating.

Or Jake had picked her up.

Yep. Jake had picked her up again.

"Put me down," she said. "I'm fine. It was just a cough."

"You're no good to us, half-dead."

"So you only want me around when I'm useful," Megan countered.

"No." He shifted her in his arms as he carried her back down the hall to her room. "But I want you better."

"I'll be fine. Just some smoke inhalation."

Amy was behind her and snorted.

Megan glared at her. "I'm fine, though. Really."

"Sure," Jake said, and he lowered her onto the hospital bed she'd been on before.

Megan grimaced.

"Enough with the cutesy shit," Eve Harrison piped up from behind Jake. "You going to tell us what happened?"

"Right," Megan said. "What do you want to know?"

"How many of them were there?" Jake asked. "What happened to Evelyn?"

"There was one. He came in the window. I don't remember every detail. Wolfs don't usually retain full memories." Flashes came to mind, images of the fight. Feelings. Nothing hard and concrete.

As was always the case when she was in wolf form.

"Just tell us what you know," Joanie said.

"He took her," Megan said. "I saw him. Just before. I'd made it out the back door. And he set the house on fire."

"He didn't kill her?" Eve asked.

Megan shook her head. "No. He took her." She shifted on the bed, her hand hitting a piece of paper, and absentmindedly, she grabbed it, hanging onto it.

"Anything else you can remember?"

"A lot of flash-steam," she said, fiddling with the paper.

A thought came to her, from before the attack. She glanced at Jake. "Did you know Evelyn could manipulate water?"

Jake stared at her. "She can what?"

Guess he didn't.

24

*J*ake was not happy.

He glared at Eve Harrison.

"Stop it. This is going to be a long fucking flight if you sit and stew all the way to eastern Europe."

"Why the hell would you leave Malcomb?"

"I told you. A job came down the pipe. I needed to leave someone to take care of a situation."

"But you left one of us. Not even two. At least leaving two would give him backup. Now we're down a man. A man who's thing is watching our backs."

If this is as ugly as she'd said it would be, why leave a man behind?

Drove Jake nuts. This is why he wanted to start being in the know. Understanding why orders were the way they were. His new mantra.

Goal in life.

Death.

Whatever.

He didn't like being in the dark.

"Trust me, we're going to need all the help we can get.

Besides, that job wasn't going to take more than one of you anyway. I made a couple calls for the situation. Malcomb's got some help if he needs it." She shook her head.

"What, do you have a goddamn army in your pocket?" Jake snapped.

"No. I have *you*," she countered. "I can't believe we're even doing this." She hit the window.

"Well, we're doing it," Jake muttered. Because he wasn't letting Evelyn get left behind. He couldn't do that to her. "If there's a chance she's still alive, we have to save her."

"If she really did kill Melios, there's a good chance she's going to make as many friends as enemies," Collins popped off from the back.

Eve nodded. "You're probably right. Unfortunately, taking out a big target makes one an even bigger target. Because if they can't take out the target, taking down the person who did, gives one just as big a name."

"Thanks for Bounty Hunting 101," Joanie muttered.

Jake bit back a smirk.

"Oh, so you all know how this shit works, well then, what am I here for?" Eve countered.

"I don't know what are you here for?" Joanie snapped back.

"Enough," Jake intervened. "Do the job, Joanie."

"Affirmative," she replied, jaw clenched.

Jake turned back to Eve. "Tell me. What do you know?"

Eve shrugged. "What I do know is the family is after her. What I don't know? That may not be her only attacker. Melios had a lot of friends. Crazy, fucked-up friends, who all thought like he did."

Jake nodded. Because he'd met a few. And they weren't all just vampires, either. "She's going to have people after her that aren't just the family."

"Probably. But she might have some friends too. Not many, but it's possible."

"We're her friends."

She glanced at him. "For now. As long as she needs you."

He raised his eyebrow. "I don't see that."

"You should. You may not have been a vampire for long, but you sure as hell have been around people long enough to know that there are always ones that use you for what they need, and then they're out."

"Is that what you're doing, Eve," Thompson asked. "Using us for what you need?"

"If that thing is a steady paycheck, then for now, yeah."

"When are you leaving?" Jake asked.

"When I'm done with you all." She glanced at her watch. "Get some rest. It'll be about dusk when we arrive."

THE SUN WAS JUST GOING down, and everything had that silvery blue glow of the night getting started.

They landed using a small, private landing strip—though it pretty much was a field. As they flew in, Jake had seen a cityscape and buildings, lit up like pinpricks of light in the night, but they moved past it to this remote place.

"I fucking hate flying," Collins muttered when they left the plane.

Jake glanced at him.

He had been awfully quiet on the flight.

"Give zero fucks," Eve replied.

Jake shook his head. "So, now what?" He asked, taking in a breath of the cold night air.

"Travel to the clan," she said. "The window to get into position is short before they are fully up and active. A lot of these old vampires don't really get around until it's full dark.

Hopefully, we can get in and out before all the family wakes up."

"Are we going to Dracula's lair?" Collins asked.

She glanced at him. "Kind of. Now, remember boys. And girl," Eve started. "They're vampires. Which means they cannot kill you. But you'd be surprised what a person can live through. Be prepared."

"Affirmative," Jake said as he pulled out the cases of toys he'd brought with him.

"There will be others there. Other species. These guys are not the only vampire clan in the world, but they are very powerful. Which means they have powerful friends. Friends who will fight for them."

"Got it."

Eve glared at him. "Whatcha got there, Reynolds?"

Jake opened his big-assed case started removing the boxes inside. "Okay, everyone. Load up."

He popped everything open for his team to take what they needed.

Joanie grinned. "Now that's pretty."

"Where the hell did you get those?" Eve asked.

Jake picked up a handgun and handed one to each of them. "Not every vampire believes in hand to hand combat, Eve."

"Damn, dude! Where did you keep those?" Collins asked.

"Where I kept the change."

Eve glanced at him. "What the fuck does that mean?"

Thompson leaned over. "Jake kept a small stash from Melios over the years, saving up whatever he thought would be useful later. If we ever found ourselves stranded, without Melios."

She raised her eyebrow. "Shit. Did you save up when you were in the military too?"

Jake shook his head. "Never thought about it then.

Learned." He clipped on weapons and ammo, and all of them packed on additional weapons—knives, some throwing blades, anything they thought they could use.

Collins clipped on a bunch of grenades.

Eve shook her head. "Fuck, give me one too."

Jake raised his eyebrow. "Really? Thought that mythicals didn't shoot guns."

She rolled her eyes. "Please. Just because it's not typical, doesn't mean it's not done. I'm quite lethal with a rifle at three hundred meters."

Jake handed her a folded-up rifle. "Let's find out."

25

*F*uck.

It really was Dracula's castle.

Sort of.

The castle, high on a hill in the middle of Romania, looked like something out of a movie or a book. The hilltop overlooked a small community that seemed to bank on the striking gothic look of the place, and as they had come through the town, the area was filled with tourist traps.

Even the streets were carting people up the hills to see the castle from all different angles.

Up to a certain point, anyway.

Roadblocks kept vehicles from getting too close, and the terrain around it would intimidate a lot of hikers.

Red rooftops, white brick, gothic elegance, and a moat. Under any other circumstances, Jake might have thought the place would be cool to visit. Just seeing it was neat.

They'd found a point in the terrain that allowed for a certain amount of observation before they made their move. Eve had managed to find some kind of floorplans for the place, but she said they were old, and couldn't be one-hundred percent relied on.

"We move in, right up that crevice there," Eve said, gesturing to an inlet on the side of the castle's wall. "Should allow us to find an entry point. It'll be tight. From there, you can search her out."

"Prisoner or guest?" Thompson asked.

"No way to tell," Eve replied.

"We'll split into groups to find her," Jake said.

"We'll need a distraction of some kind," Eve said. "Something to keep the guards busy."

"Look, wolves on the roof," Joanie said.

Eve nodded. "Yep. Count six."

"What is that over there?" Joanie asked gesturing to the man on the far corner. "Fuck. He's cute."

Eve shifted to look at the mythical in question. "I do believe, kids, that is your dragon. Check the ears, and that wave of heat coming off him."

"I'll take him out." Thompson pulled out his gun, steadying it across the rocks. "I can probably hit him."

"You may not have to," Eve said. She adjusted her binoculars. "I can't make it out for sure. Speaking Russian. I think that he's saying some debt is paid, though."

"Makes sense, with the whole housekeeping thing," Jake said. Paid to do a job? Then he'd likely be gone when it was done.

"Who is that joining him?" Joanie asked.

Eve gritted her teeth. "Sir Richard? What the actual fuck. Seriously, that damn boy."

Richard crossed to the dragon, and it looked like they were having a rather intense conversation. Finger jabs and wild hand gestures and all.

She glanced at Jake. "You all move in. I'll be right back."

Jake opened his mouth to argue, but Eve was too quick. She disappeared.

And reappeared on the other rooftop, right in between Richard and the dragon.

"So why doesn't she do that for us?"

"Shit, that's why," Collins said, pointing to the side of the building.

Like an eruption, mythicals burst from the building's walls, including from the crevices that they were going to try and sneak into, and they converged on the rooftop.

"Fuck, she tripped an alarm," Joanie said. "Come on, boys. Let's move."

"Let's practice those leaps," Jake said. "Priority—get Evelyn. Everything else is secondary."

"Roger that."

"Move!"

26

"What are you doing here?" Richard demanded. "You were supposed to be back in Liverly, protecting the girl."

"I didn't say I'd do anything for you!" Eve yelled back at Richard

"She's here, right in the middle of my damn negotiations."

"Well, at least she's alive," Eve said, hoping her vampires were listening. "Did they lock her up? Put her in prison so she could rot? Or are they just going to kill her?"

"She's in a lovely suite," the dragon added. "Kept safe."

Eve and Richard glanced at the dragon. "Pardon?" Eve said.

"It was a foolish endeavor to hide her from me," the dragon said. "No one stops a Kuznetsov dragon from his prize."

"Stuff it, fire boy," Eve snapped and turned to Richard. "If you would have fucking told me who she was, this whole thing could have been avoided."

The alarms were blaring, and out of the woodwork, came vampires. A-friggin' lot of them.

Eve wound up being back to back with Richard.

"Great. You have probably ruined everything," Richard said as he pulled his sword and started fighting.

"If you and your goddamn Templars had actually been straight up, things may not have happened." Eve pulled her own katanas.

"What do you want us to do, become an oversharing Facebook poster?"

Ash flew in the air.

"Wouldn't hurt," Eve said. More ash flew through the air.

Gunshots echoed in the night.

Ahh, the kids pulled their pistols, Eve thought. The echoes punctuated the fighting on the roof with Eve and Richard.

"Who has guns?" Richard snapped.

Eve grinned. "Ahh, my kids."

"Of course. Didn't you teach them anything?" Swing of his sword and ash exploded.

Even swung her weapons around and got the same pretty ash. "Believe it or not, they did that on their own."

Then she started getting hot.

But not in a good way.

Over her shoulder, the dragon had somehow ended up in their little circle. "What the fuck, dude?"

"Prince Maksim Kuznetsov was just leaving," Richard said. "This chaos is all you, Eve."

"Just the way I like it," she snapped back.

Richard grumbled, and took out his frustration on some attacking vampires.

"I will return to my people, my family's debt paid." He paused, gesturing out toward the surrounding land around the castle. "What is that?"

Eve glanced at the area and couldn't help smiling. "That, boys, is what we're distracting the castle from."

There on the land, leaping away from the castle, was

Reynolds and the rest of team, shadows in the night, and with what looked to be a girl in his arms, racing away.

"It was almost too easy," she said.

And then she saw a massive shift in the land, shadows coming to life all around the team as they raced toward their rendezvous.

They were being herded into a trap.

"Don't think your distraction worked, Eve," Richard said.

She glared at him. "Hold your breath."

She grabbed his arm and stepped through the sheldevak room—the portal that made stepping in and out of the mortal realm so easy.

Because her team needed backup.

27

*B*efore he realized what was happening, the trap had been sprung.

It had been way too easy to get Evelyn. They literally walked in, found her almost immediately, and then took off.

Evelyn went with them like she'd been waiting for them.

But not in the trapped, prisoner way.

Every step, though, felt wrong. From the moment they hit the castle, it felt too simple. Why was she there, sitting in a chair, looking bored, almost just waiting for them?

What was the purpose? They were there to save her, but really, she didn't look like she needed saving. Her only injury was a bandage on her arm; otherwise, she was the picture of health. They had to run for it because he knew this was bad. He felt it in his bones.

Like really bad.

And this escape? This was worse. The trap slammed them hard. They had so been played.

But why?

And by who?

"We're surrounded," Jake said, as he looked over the

ground. A smallish clearing, water to one side, a cliff face to the other, and more mountainside to traverse if they moved forward.

"Hold here?" Thompson asked.

"Look lively, they're coming soon," Jake said.

Evelyn looked around. "This will work," she said.

Jake glanced at her. "Evelyn."

She pulled away from him. "Yeah, this will work nicely."

He glanced at the girl, who didn't look like a kid, not the way she was standing. "What is going on, Evelyn."

"You can come out now," she said.

Jake looked around.

From the woods came multiple vampires. All of them old.

Several looked a helluva lot like Melios.

Well, we found the family.

One, in particular, came out, front and center. "You must be Melios's," the man said, sort of gruff. He shook his head. "Impudent boy." The last seemed more for himself than for Jake's ears.

"What is this," Jake asked, though his gaze landed on Evelyn more than the older man. "What have you done, Evelyn?"

She blinked. "What I had to do." Her eyes—those damn purple eyes of hers—were void of emotion.

Jake's gaze darted to his team. And he wanted to kick his own ass. He realized what was going on, and he was sick. She'd played him.

Hard. This kid had absolutely played him like a fiddle, gave him all the signs that she was this sweet kid who needed someone to protect her.

"Guys," Jake said as the trees started to move with even more vampires coming out of the woods.

"Don't worry," Joanie said. "We'll kill you later for the *SNAFU.*" She held her gun up, ready to shoot.

"Who the hell are you?" Collins asked, his own guns up.

"You don't know?"

"I like to know who I'm going to kill," Collins replied.

He smirked. "Don Romano, leader of the Romano clan. Melios's father."

"Ugliness runs in the family," Collins replied.

He sneered. "My son never was good at choosing who to sire."

"Come on, Evelyn," Jake said. "Let's go home."

The girl shook her head. "Maybe I already am."

"This is not your home," Jake said. "Your home is with me."

She took a few steps toward Don Romano.

"Best to not try and negotiate," Romano said. "The child is doing what Melios told her. She's surviving."

"How did you know we'd come?" Jake asked.

She rolled her eyes. "Really? Of course, you would come. You'd save your precious little Evelyn. Kid. Child. Whatever you call me. After all, I'd bring you food. Help you when you were hurt." She said it all with a whine, mocking him. "Did it never dawn on you that I was playing all of you?"

Jake couldn't believe it. "You lied about everything."

She smiled. "It's what I do best."

He stepped closer to the girl. "Today, she survives because she turned you over."

"She lied to you, then, and you bought it," Jake said. "Just like she lied to everyone else."

"I didn't lie," she said. "The truth worked so much better this time."

"You didn't even kill Melios. It was a Templar Knight who did it," Jake said.

"No, I did it!" she fired back. "I buried that stake into his heart, and he disappeared into a thousand pieces right there in front of me."

"Bullshit," Collins yelled back, mimicking a horn.

"You're not strong enough," Jake said. Over her shoulder, where the water churned down the side of the mountain, he saw the water moving.

Bending toward her.

"Oh, she killed him. Of that I have no doubt," Romano said, patting the girl's arm. "She did what she had to, so she survived. Tomorrow, she may take down a dragon family, something I'd hoped she'd do today. But that's neither here nor there. We'll take out those flying idiots soon enough."

A glow in the sky was their only warning.

The dragon landed with a crash, right in the middle of the gathering.

"You *wanted* me to kill a child," the dragon said. "To break my family code and honor."

"Of course. What's more important, your title, or your honor?" Romano said.

"You had no right to manipulate the Kuznetsov Family like this." The dragon's body was getting hotter and hotter by the moment, glowing like fire.

"You were hired to fulfill a promise. To do a task for the Romano Clan. And you failed."

"I brought you the child."

"You didn't kill her."

"Dragons do not kill children!"

And the fire exploded from him. '

About the same time water burst from the waterfall, toward the dragon, pushed by Evelyn's hand gestures

Jake inhaled a breath just before the smoke hit him.

And suddenly, everything went very, very white as the flash-steam exploded all around him.

28

*J*ake hit the concrete floor hard.

So did the rest of the team, quickly, one right after the other. A pop in and out, in a flash, they were all there.

Minus Evelyn, anyway.

But plus, a dragon.

"Dude, the dragon burned me," Joanie said, groaning as she rolled over.

Jake shook his head. "What the actual fuck?" He glanced around.

They were back.

In Jackstone. In a workout gym.

Eve stood over them. "Everyone okay?"

"Fuck," Collins said and threw up.

"Sorry, Travis. That happens when non-sheldevak travel the sheldevak way," Eve said with a laugh.

"And tell me why we didn't travel that way to the castle in the first place?" Jake muttered.

"I can't go anywhere I've never seen in person."

Sir Richard was there as well, rubbing his temple.

"Collins is fine," Joanie said with a laugh.

"I am sorry," the dragon said. He stared at Joanie. "Thank you for grabbing me."

Joanie shrugged. "I may need a favor someday."

The dragon put his hand to his heart. "On this day, I, Prince Maksim of Kuznetsov Family owe a debt of honor to you, Joanie,

"Joanie Alekhine," she replied.

His eyebrow raised. "You are of Russian descent?"

She nodded.

"Then I am dually honored to give you, Joanie Alekhine, vampire clan of…" he glanced at her, then at the rest of them. "What clan are you?"

Jake glanced at Eve.

"Jackstone Vampires, Harrison Division," Jake said.

Everyone smiled.

"That'll work." Eve Harrison said. She pointed at Jake. "And now you'll do as I say?"

Jake shrugged. "If you tell me why."

"Maybe."

"Then, maybe."

They shook hands.

He guessed it might have been the best he was going to get out of Eve Harrison.

29

*M*egan ran down the hallway.
He's back.
He's back.
He's back.

She knocked on the door where Jake had been sharing the room with the kid, the door was shut, and she pounded on it, clenched in her fist a piece of paper.

The paper had fallen out of Jake's pocket or something in the hospital. She'd been playing with it before when they were talking, but she fell asleep and didn't really mess with it until after the full moon. She had to go straight from the hospital to her cage, to make sure she didn't turn into a werewolf and ravage the city or something.

Someone had put the note with her things. Amy probably.

So she only just read it when she got dressed. She'd seen the writing and thought it was Jake's.

She'd opened it up, in case there was something in it he needed while he was going to rescue Evelyn.

But it wasn't what she thought.

It wasn't plans or anything helpful for Evelyn.

It was a list of reasons why she and Jake could be together. How a werewolf and a vampire could make it.

Case studies.

Like the couple in Kent, back in the 1700s, where they were soul mates, the wolf imprinted on the vampire, and they stayed together for the wolf's entire life, and then when the wolf died, the vampire died as well.

A very famous case of inter-species mixing.

But he also listed multiple cases, over centuries, where werewolves and vampires had made lives together.

Each word she read, crumbled the wall in her heart a bit more. Because so much of her hesitation was about him being immortal, and that she wouldn't be.

The last bit, though, was what got her the most.

I can't say that I would go on. Hell, I can't say that this would work out at all. But I'm willing to commit. If you are willing to. It may have been one night.

But, Megan, I need you.

Forever.

Please.

She'd stared at that.

Read it over and over.

And knew she had to get to him now. To talk to him. To see him.

She pounded on the door again.

"Jake! Open up!"

There was no answer inside.

"Please, Jake! Open up."

Still no response.

"I'm not leaving. I need to talk to you."

She sighed and slumped to the floor. "I was wrong, Jake. I was so wrong." She leaned against the door, clenching the piece of paper. "I thought it was just my beast. My wolf, trying to talk to me, because I didn't want to think that a vampire would be my soul mate. Hell, if my clan were alive, they'd probably shun me forever for it. But I don't care. Not anymore."

She unfolded the paper again. "I don't want to lose you. I think I love you too."

"Well, that's good, because I don't want to be here without you," Jake said.

She jerked and looked over her shoulder. "Jake, but… What?"

"I was down the hall, moving my stuff back to the original room."

"What about Evelyn?"

"She's gone."

She covered her mouth. "I'm sorry."

He shook his head. "She's not dead. She's gone. She is with Melios's clan. I don't know what they're going to do with her, but I can't imagine it'll be good."

She held up her hand, and Jake helped her stand. And in doing so, he pulled her into an embrace. "Now, what was it you were saying?"

"That I'm an idiot."

He raised his eyebrow. "I don't think either of us have been very smart in the last few days."

"I don't think so, either," she said.

He held her to him, their lips very close. "Let's say we start again. Hi. I'm Jake."

"I'm Megan."

"I really want to make love to you."

She shook her head. "No."

"Why not?"

"Because, honey, werewolves don't make love."

"What do you do?"

"We fuck."

"I'll take it."

EPILOGUE

*E*velyn looked around the castle bedroom.

"Huh," she said. "This is where Melios grew up?"

"His very room," Dom Romano said. He said it with a kind of stuck-up pride that bored Evelyn.

It was just a room.

She glanced from shelf to shelf. There were books all around. Lots of old stuff and the smell was in the air.

That old, musty smell.

"He used to say that I was going to change the world."

Dom Romano nodded. "Only descendants of the First Vampire look like you."

She nodded. "Melios used to say that all the time. Bored me then. Still bores me now."

"Why?"

She turned and looked at him. "Lineage means nothing unless there's the power to back it up."

"This clan has power."

"I sure hope so," Evelyn said.

"Miss Evelyn, we have more power than most."

She shook her head. "No."

"I can assure you, Miss Evelyn, that we have power."

"No. I don't want to be Evelyn anymore."

He raised his bushy eyebrow. "Oh?"

"I think I need a queenlier name." Her finger scraped the spine of a book on the shelf. One name on it popped out. "Victoria." She faced Romano again. "I shall be Victoria."

"As you wish."

She nodded.

Because she was going to be his queen. And the queen of the rest of the vampires. All it was going to take was resources. A lot of resources.

And so far, it looked like the Romano clan had it.

DEAR READER

I hope you enjoyed Vampires Don't Babysit. I know I enjoyed writing it. I always wondered what happened to Melios's Vampire Seals that he had when I wrote the Mythical Knights Series.

Word-of-mouth is crucial for any author to succeed in the publishing industry. If you enjoyed this book, please consider leaving a review. Even just a couple of lines really help.

Sign up for my newsletter, at CandiceGilmer.com where I send out excerpts, cover reveals, and the latest release information.

TURN THE PAGE

For a special excerpt of
Vampires Don't Protect
Book 2

VAMPIRES DON'T PROTECT

BOOK 2 IN THE VAMPIRE MYTHICALS SERIES

*B*eing a vampire sounded like fun.
Up all night.

Sleep all day.

Drink the blood of thine enemy.

Whatever the hell that was.

Yeah. It all sounded fun. Hell of a lot better than being shot at or being bombed. Or expected to obey without thinking.

Then Isaac Malcomb became a vampire.

And he learned really quickly that it wasn't nearly as much fun as he thought it would be. What with the whole obeying, starving, and exhaustion.

And the immortal.

Like forever, he would be like this.

That was really going to suck.

Both literally and figuratively.

Far too many times, Malcomb watched his sire roll around with humans, fuck them, eat them—not the sexual way, either—then discard the bodies.

Blood everywhere.

Starving, his head throbbed with hunger he'd hear the heartbeats of the dying victims as Melios fed.

And his sire would expect him to stand there as a guard. Watch. But not move.

Because it amused the fucker.

If Malcomb was lucky, Melios would have thrown him an arm or something to drain the last of the blood out.

He wasn't always lucky.

Especially not now. The hunger pulsed under his skin, and it put him on edge. Like pretty much all of them. And there were a lot down here.

Surrounded by a room full of smelly, stinking vampires, midafternoon was when everyone should be sleeping. Instead, they were gathered around a table—like a war room in most respects.

It kind of was a war room.

It's where he and the rest of his little squad of vampires got their orders.

The building in downtown Liverly that Melios had commandeered to make his nest sat among a half-dozen other old or beaten down buildings. An abandoned warehouse that no one paid any attention to on the river. They kept tearing down the notices of the upcoming auction at Melios's request. Maybe the vampire thought if he removed them, no one would know the building will be sold at auction in a couple months.

The only people who came down there were local independent filmmakers and photographers who wanted a depressed, dramatic background. It didn't take much to scare them off.

Or have a meal. Either worked.

If Melios was feeling generous. Most of the time, though he wasn't. He kept all the new blood for himself. The rest of them got scraps.

"Gather," Melios said. Lean and slender, he had a particular other-worldly look. Like he wasn't from the neighborhood. He held out his hands, and it was almost hypnotic, watching the way he'd move.

All the vampires circled their master. Melios had sired every single one in the room. There were more that weren't in the nest, however many he'd made around the world in his multiple-century existence.

Malcomb, like all the others, were newer to being a vampire. And everyone stood elbow to elbow, waited to hear what was coming.

The whole place was electrified with anticipation. They all could feel it.

Malcomb could really feel it. On top of the hunger, this anticipation seemed to radiate off some.

He glanced at Jake Reynolds, his friend.

Commanding officer.

But a friend first. Sort of.

His face was neutral, and he didn't seem to know what was going on either. No one seemed aware.

Except maybe Washington. But Washington always looked like he knew what was going on, whether he did or not.

Melios's gaze passed over them all. "An attack is imminent. The Templars are moving on me and my nest. I imagine they will arrive at dark. Chivalry at its finest," Melios snorted.

Malcomb resisted the urge to roll his eyes. Stupid, really. He would have attacked while the vampires were at their weakest—during the day when they couldn't go outside.

Advantage of the situation, and all that.

Melios glanced at Malcomb, then to Reynolds. "SEALS, defend me."

"Yes, sir!" Malcomb replied, along with Reynolds, Joanie

Alekhine, Travis Collins, Thompson—Malcomb could never remember his first name. Something weird. And of course, Deke Smith. The monster of the squad.

That was just Reynold's squad. Men, and a woman, that he'd personally brought into the nest—he'd been the one to recruit them all.

Melios kept two other squads as well, and all former military or police of some sort. He liked having vampires who had extensive training in their mortal life, and the old sire used them for whatever operation he had going on.

And he always seemed to have something going on. Some kind of mission or intel he wanted to know.

The rest of the vampires around the group—the ones who had been turned, and just wound up being dangerous because they were a little extra crazy—were assigned to work in different areas.

The three squads, however, quickly planned out a defensive strategy.

"Reynolds, you take yours over to the south wall, wait for engagement."

Reynolds nodded.

"Brooks, you go north." Washington, the oldest of all of them, one of a handful of Vietnam vets among them, "We'll take the frontal assault."

"Didn't you all learn anything from Vietnam?" Malcomb popped off.

Washington glared at him.

Malcomb blinked.

Washington was on him. "Do *not* speak of what you do not know."

Slam.

Slam.

Boom.

Malcomb shoved him off. "Get over it!"

Malcomb looked for bruises that should have been there, some evidence of side of the fight, but Washington's brown skin looked unmarred.

The big vampire leaped into the air, hovered for a second, and landed again, right in front of Malcomb.

"Your mouth will get you ashed, dumb assed SEAL." And boom, he slammed Malcomb upside the head.

It was so fast, Isaac didn't see it coming.

"What the fuck?" He rubbed his head. "And I'm not a goddamn SEAL!"

"Here, you are," Washington said, glaring first at Malcomb, then at everyone. "Fall out, everyone."

The room echoed in affirmatives.

Washington glared at Reynolds. "Control your squad, or after this, I'll see they meet a goddamn stake."

"Yes, sir," Reynolds replied.

Washington put his back to him and walked away.

Reynolds glanced at Malcomb.

And hit him upside the head.

"Jesus, fuck," Malcomb said. "Do you fucking mind?"

"What the hell is wrong with you?" Reynolds fired.

"He's a dumb ass, as usual," Deke piped up.

"I didn't see you helping me."

Deke shrugged. "You're an idiot to challenge Washington."

"I wasn't challenging him. I just wanted to know—"

"Yeah, we got it," Joanie said. "You're not funny, Malcomb."

"It was kinda funny," Collins said.

"Thanks for the support," Malcomb replied.

Joanie elbowed Collins. He shrugged and grinned, his elongated teeth peeking out over his bottom lip.

Thompson shook his head. "Regardless, we have Immortal Templar Knights en route for, what, exactly?"

"Does it matter?" Reynolds asked.

"Kind of," Malcomb replied. In the military, the real military, Malcomb never questioned anything. And he wound up occasionally doing some sketchy shit in the name of orders.

He didn't like it then.

Still didn't.

"We follow orders, and worry about it later," Reynolds said. "Doesn't matter why they're coming, just that they are, and they'll destroy every one of us." Reynolds glared at him. "You know that."

Malcomb nodded. Because he did.

The Immortal Knights Templar took no prisoners. They would rather kill a mythical over questioning them. And if they did hold one and not kill him? He'd wind up dead as soon as he was no longer useful.

"They're coming for the woman," came a kid's voice.

They all turned to look.

In the corner, was the kid. Age undetermined, exactly, she was somewhere between twelve and fifteen—petite, with bright purple eyes. One minute, like now, she'd look innocent and sweet, and more like a kid than anything. Then there were other times, she didn't.

And she scared the fuck out of Malcomb. Vampires smelled bad. It was the lust and blood, Malcomb had figured out.

She, however, was different.

He didn't know why. She just gave off a different vibe than anyone he'd ever met. He didn't know if that was good or bad.

She was Melios's little pet he was raising. No one really knew why.

She, however, seemed to like the squad. Or just Reynolds.

She'd never elaborated on her infatuation, and Isaac wasn't going to ask.

Malcomb glanced around, and in the distance, he heard it —before he hadn't noticed, but sure enough, he could hear someone in the room beyond the one they were in. He took a deep breath.

He could smell the human. Her sweat. And her fear.

Chains tinkled.

"Who is she?"

The kid shrugged. "Doesn't matter. Melios thinks she's important."

"Do you?" Joanie asked.

She shook her head. "Here," she said and sat down a big cup on the ground before Reynolds.

One of Melios's drinking chalices. The ones he kept under a tap of blood in his main room upstairs.

Reynolds raised his eyebrow, and everyone's stomachs growled a little.

"You need to eat before," she said.

"Before what?" Malcomb asked.

She turned her purple eyes on him.

"Before they come and kill everyone."

Malcomb repressed a shudder.

Reynolds nodded. "Thank you."

She smiled. "Don't die."

"We'll try not to, kid."

She smiled, waved, and snuck back up to wherever it was she was supposed to be.

Now Available

ABOUT THE AUTHOR

USA Today and *NY Times* bestselling author Candice Gilmer leads a dangerous double life as a mommy and a writer. In between boo-boo healing and fixing broken toys, she writes stories usually to the tune of children's television shows.

Her books range from vampires and werewolves to mermaids and fairies to contemporary and fairy tale romances--a huge variety, just like her broad, geek-girl heart. She adores *Star Wars, Star Trek*, Marvel, and DC, (you CAN love them all), and her hero will always be Captain America.

Growing up in the Midwest, Candice stays close to her family, especially the ones with basements when the tornadoes come around.

All in all, she stays very busy, but really, she wouldn't have it any other way.

Well, maybe a little less children's television.

Follow and keep up with Candice

facebook.com/candicegilmerauthor
twitter.com/candicegilmer
instagram.com/candicegilmerauthor
bookbub.com/authors/candice-gilmer

OTHER BOOKS BY CANDICE GILMER

Paranormal Romances

Guys & Godmothers

The Magic Under His Nose (#1) – This Fairy Godmother has her work cut out for her.

Magic Right Before His Eyes (#2) – Can her magic save his bad decision and bring him his Happily Ever After?

Magic That's Just His Taste (#3) – Magic be damned, she was making this Happily Ever After work, because he deserves it.

The Mythicals

Saving Her Destiny (#1) Sometimes the future comes knocking. Sometimes it knocks you into next week.

Guarding Her Secret (#2) -- Sometimes, to protect the monster, the rules have to be broken.

The Mythical Knights

Brightest Shadow (#1) The darkest shadows sometimes have the brightest moments.

Dark Within (#2) There are monsters, then there are monsters. Which kind wants her dead?

Not a Gentleman's Christmas (A Holiday Story) She thought a gentleman would save her. He's no gentleman.

Bravest Flame (#3) All it takes is a spark...

Darker Cravings (#4) She wanted it hot. But is two too hot to handle?

Darkest Judgment (#5) In the heat of the moment, a Templar's judgment is his last hope.

Vampire Mythicals

Vampires Don't Babysit (#1) Surviving should have been enough. It wasn't.

Vampires Don't Protect (#2) He should be terrorizing. Instead, he's protecting.

Vampires Don't Date the Boss (#3) Find the relics. Save the world. Don't fall for the boss. Check. Check. Well...

Vampires Don't Fall in Love (#4) He burns for her, but will his fire turn her to ash?

Elemental Mythicals

Can't Remember Dick (#1) They stole her sister's soul, and now Aria has to remember her past to save her sister's future.

Sci-Fi Romance

Galaxy Storm Series

The Temptress's Cyborg (#1) She followed her emperor's orders, but this cyborg makes her question everything.

The Lady's Cyborg (#2) She did her duty, bowing to her princess, but when she's left to her own wits, this lady finds herself along and in danger, with a cyborg.

The Mistress's Cyborg (#3) There is nothing she has never handled, as the emperor's mistress, she has to convince this cyborg that peace is worth the war.

The Virgin's Cyborg (#4) As the spare, she was expected to learn, but not perform. When mistaken for the princess, she vows to make sure her sister is kept safe, all in the name of the Terran Empire.

The Princess's Cyborg (#5) Rescued by a tarnished cyborg, she must get back to their settlement and secure peace, before her own people tear it apart.

Most Wanted Alien Brides

(Intergalactic Dating Agency)

Slammer

Hard Time

Solitary

Fairy Tale Romance

The Charming Fairy Tales

Out of the Tower (#1) He thought he was rescuing her from the tower, but truly, his heart was the one in danger.

Slipping Away (#2) He didn't want any responsibility or commitment. His heart had other ideas.

Ending The Curse (#3) Honoring promises was what a nobleman did, even when his heart tells him different.

Contemporary Romance

Barrum, Ks Romances

Fantasy Girl – His fantasies will kill her.

The Reluctant Prince -- Duty comes with a price—his heart.

Mission of Christmas – This year, he was going to give her what she really needed—a real Christmas.

His Velvet Touch -- He was going to use her, but he didn't expect to need her

Celestial Springs Salon, Part of Barrum, Ks

Summer Burns (#1) – He was only supposed to check on her. Not fall for her.

Autumn Falls (#2) -- The last thing she wants may be exactly what she needs.

Winter Chills (#3) -- Letting go has never been so hard. Or so incredible.

For excerpts and the latest information, check out

WWW.CANDICEGILMER.COM

Made in the USA
Middletown, DE
02 July 2023